Seth moved slowly toward her, with both arms extended.

Tabby had an overwhelming desire to rush into those strong arms and declare her undying love, but she held herself in check, remembering the little scene she'd encountered when she first entered Seth's shop. It was obvious that Seth had more than a business relationship with Cheryl.

Seth kept moving closer, until she could feel his warm breath on her upturned face. She trembled and her eyelids drifted shut. Tabby knew she shouldn't let Seth kiss her—not when he was seeing someone else. Her heart said something entirely different, though, and it was with her whole heart that Tabby offered her lips willingly to Seth's inviting kiss.

She relished in the warmth of Seth's embrace, until the sharp ringing of the telephone pulled them apart.

"Uh, guess I'd better get that," Seth mumbled. He stepped away from Tabby and moved across the room toward the desk where the phone sat.

Tabby looked down at Rosie and muttered, "I think I was just saved by the bell."

WANDA E. BRUNSTETTER lives in a small town in central Washington. Together, she and her husband, Richard, a pastor, have a puppet ministry they often share at other churches, Bible camps, and Bible schools. Wanda has been a ventriloquist for twenty years and has taught classes and written many articles on the subject of ventriloquism. She welcomes you to visit her web site at: http://hometown.aol.com/rlbweb/index.html, where you can see some of her ventriloquist figures.

HEARTSONG PRESENTS

Books by Wanda E. Brunstetter
HP253—A Merry Heart
HP421—Looking for a Miracle

Talking
for Two

Wanda E. Brunstetter

Heartsong Presents

To my son, Richard, Jr.,
who first suggested I learn ventriloquism.
To my daughter, Lorine,
the best ventriloquist student I ever had.
To Clinton Detweiler,
a talented ventriloquist:
Much thanks for all your helpful insights.

A note from the author:
*I love to hear from my readers! You may correspond with me
by writing:* **Wanda E. Brunstetter**
Author Relations
PO Box 719
Uhrichsville, OH 44683

ISBN 1-58660-481-3

TALKING FOR TWO

All Scripture quotations, unless otherwise indicated, are taken from
the HOLY BIBLE, NEW INTERNATIONAL VERSION ®. NIV ®. Copyright ©
1973, 1978, 1984 by International Bible Society. Used by permis-
sion of Zondervan Publishing House. All rights reserved.

All of the characters and events in this book are fictitious. Any
resemblance to actual persons, living or dead, or to actual events
is purely coincidental.

Cover illustration by Randy Hamblin.

PRINTED IN THE U.S.A.

one

"Miss Johnson, will you make Roscoe talk to us again?" Four-year-old Ricky Evans squinted his pale blue eyes and offered up a toothy grin so appealing that Tabitha knew it would be impossible for her to say no.

She pulled the floppy-eared dog puppet from its home in the bottom drawer of her desk and quickly inserted her hand. Thankful she was wearing blue jeans and not a dress today, she dropped to her knees and hid behind the desk, bringing only the puppet into view. Roscoe let out a couple of loud barks, which brought several more children running to see the program. Then Tabitha launched into her routine.

"Did you know I used to belong to a flea circus?" the scruffy-looking puppet asked. The children now sat on the floor, completely mesmerized, waiting for what was to come next.

"Really and truly?" a young girl called out.

Roscoe's dark head bobbed up and down. "That's right, and before long, I ran away and stole that whole itchy show!"

The children giggled, and Roscoe howled in response.

Tabitha smiled to herself. She was always glad for the chance to entertain the day care kids, even if she was doing it behind a desk, with a puppet that looked like he'd seen better days.

Five minutes and several jokes later, she ended her routine and sent all the children to their tables for a snack of chocolate-chip cookies and milk.

"You're really good with that goofy puppet," came a woman's soft voice behind her.

Tabitha turned to face her coworker and best friend, Donna

5

Hartley. "I enjoy making the kids laugh," she said, pushing an irritating strand of hair away from her face. "It makes me feel like I'm doing something meaningful."

Always confident, always consoling, Donna offered her a bright smile. "Just helping me run Caring Christian Day Care is meaningful."

Tabitha blinked. "You really think so?"

Donna pulled out a chair and motioned Tabitha to do the same. "You know what you need, Tabby?"

Tabitha took a seat and offered up a faint smile, relishing the warm, familiar way her friend said her nickname. Donna began calling her that when she and her parents moved next door to the Johnsons, nearly twenty-three years ago. That was when Tabitha had been a happy, outgoing child. That was when she'd been an only child.

Shortly after she turned six, her whole life suddenly changed. The birth of blond-haired, blue-eyed sister Lois, had turned talkative, confident Tabby into a timid, stuttering, introverted child. Her father, who'd once doted on her, now had eyes only for the little girl who looked so much like him. Tabby's mother was a meek, subservient woman; rather than stand up to her controlling husband and his blatant acts of favoritism, she had merely chosen to keep silent while Tabby turned into a near recluse.

"Are you listening to me?" Donna asked, jerking Tabby's thoughts back to the present.

"Huh? What were you saying?"

"Do you know what you need?"

Tabby drew in a deep breath and blew it out quickly. "No, but I'm sure you can't wait to tell me."

Donna snickered. "Okay, so I'm not able to keep my big mouth shut where you're concerned. Old habits die hard, you know."

Tabby tapped her foot impatiently. "So, what do I need?"

"You need to attend that Christian workers' conference we heard about a few weeks ago."

"You know I don't do well in crowds," Tabby grumbled. "Especially with a bunch of strangers. I stutter whenever I talk to anyone but you or the day care kids, and—"

"But you won't be in a crowd," Donna reminded. "You'll be in a workshop, learning puppetry. You can hide behind a puppet box."

Tabby shrugged, letting her gaze travel to the group of happy children sitting at the table across the room. "No promises, but I'll think about it."

≥

Seth Beyers had never figured out why anyone would want to buy an ugly dummy, but the customer he was waiting on right now wanted exactly that.

"The uglier the better," the young man said with a deep chuckle. "The audiences at the clubs where I often perform seem to like ugly and crude."

Seth had been a Christian for more than half of his twenty-six years, and he'd been interested in ventriloquism nearly that long as well. It just didn't set right with him when someone used a God-given talent to fill people's heads with all kinds of garbage. While most of Seth's customers were Christians, a few secular people, like Alan Capshaw, came to his shop to either purchase a ventriloquist dummy or have one repaired.

"Okay, I'll do my best for ugly," Seth said with a slight nod. "How does Dumbo ears, a long nose, and lots of freckles sound?"

"The big ears and extended nose is fine, but skip the freckles and stick a big ugly wart on the end of the dummy's snout." Alan grinned, revealing a set of pearly white teeth.

The dummy may turn out ugly, but this guy must really attract women, Seth mentally noted. Alan Capshaw not only had perfect teeth, but his slightly curly blond hair, brilliant blue eyes, and muscular body made Seth feel like he was the ugly dummy. He never could figure out why he'd been cursed with red hair and a slender build.

Seth waited until the self-assured customer placed a sizable down payment on his dummy order and sauntered out the door—and then he allowed himself the privilege of self-analysis. Sure, he'd had a few girlfriends over the past several years, and if he were really honest with himself, he guessed maybe he wasn't too bad looking, either. *At least not compared to the ugly dummy I'll soon be constructing.*

Whenever Seth went anywhere with his little buddy, Rudy Right, folks of all ages seemed to flock around him. Of course, he was pretty sure it was the winking dummy to whom they were actually drawn and not the hopeful ventriloquist.

Seth scratched the back of his head and moved over to the workbench. This was the place where he felt most comfortable. This was where he could become so engrossed in work that his troubles were left behind. He'd started fooling around with a homemade sock puppet and a library book on ventriloquism soon after he was old enough to read. When he turned twelve, his parents enrolled him in a home-study course on ventriloquism. In no time at all, Seth Beyers, normal, active teenager, had turned into a humorous, much sought-after ventriloquist. It wasn't long after that when he began performing at local fairs, school functions, and numerous church programs. About that time, he also decided he would like to learn how to make and repair dummies for a living. He'd always been good with his hands, and with a little help from a couple of books, it didn't take long before he completed his first ventriloquist figure.

Seth now owned and operated his own place of business, and people from all over the United States either brought or sent their ventriloquist figures to him for repairs. When he wasn't performing or teaching a class on ventriloquism, Seth filled special orders for various kinds of dummies. All but one of Seth's goals had been reached.

He wanted a wife and family. He'd been raised as an only child and had always longed for brothers and sisters. Instead of playing with a sibling, Seth's best friend was his sock puppet. Then Mom and Dad had been killed in a plane crash when he was fourteen, and he'd been forced to move from Seattle to Tacoma to live with Grandpa and Grandma Beyers. He loved them both a lot, but it wasn't the same as having his own family. Besides, his grandparents were getting on in years and wouldn't be around forever.

Seth groaned and reached for a piece of sandpaper to begin working on a wooden leg. "What I really need is to find someone who shares my love for Christ and wants to serve Him the way I do." He shook his head. "I wonder if such a woman even exists."

The telephone rang, pulling him out of his reflections. He reached for it quickly, before the answering machine had a chance to click on. "Beyers' Ventriloquist Studio." Seth frowned as he listened. "Glen Harrington's had a family emergency and you want me to fill in?" There was a long pause. "Yeah, I suppose I could work it into my schedule."

Seth wrote down a few particulars, then hung up the phone. The last thing he needed was another seminar to teach, but he didn't have the heart to say no. He'd check his notes from the workshop he'd done in Portland a few months ago, and if everything seemed up to date, maybe there wouldn't be too much preliminary work. Since the seminar was only for one day, he was sure he could make the time.

He closed his eyes briefly as his lips curled into a smile. *Who knows, maybe I'll be able to help some young, talented kid hone his skills and use ventriloquism as a tool to serve the Lord.*

Tabby stared dismally out the living room window in the converted garage apartment she shared with Donna. It was raining again, but then this was late spring, and she did live in the suburbs of Tacoma, Washington. Liquid sunshine was a common occurrence here in the beautiful Evergreen State.

Normally the rain didn't bother her much, but on this particular Saturday, it seemed as though every drop of water falling outside was landing on her instead of on the emerald grass and budding trees. She felt as if it were filling up her soul with agonizing depression and loneliness.

Tabby wrapped her arms tightly around her chest, as a deep moan escaped her lips. "Maybe I should have gone to Seattle with Donna and her parents after all." She shivered involuntarily. Tabby disliked crowds, and there was always a huge flock of people at the Seattle Center. No, she was better off here at home, even if she was lonely and miserable.

A sharp rap on the front door brought Tabby's musings to a halt. She moved away from the window and shuffled toward the sound. Standing on tiptoes, she peered through the small peephole, positioned much too high for her short stature.

Tabby's heart took a dive, and her stomach churned like whipping cream about to become butter. She didn't receive many surprise visits from her sister. Maybe this one would go better than the last. At least she hoped it would. Tabby drew in a deep breath, grasped the door handle, then yanked it open.

A blond-haired, blue-eyed beauty, holding a black, rain-soaked umbrella and ensconced in a silver gray raincoat, greeted her with a wide smile. "Hi, Timid Tabitha. How's everything going?"

Tabby stepped aside as Lois rushed in, giving her umbrella a good shake and scattering droplets of cold water all over Tabby's faded blue jeans. Lois snapped the umbrella closed and dropped it into the wrought-iron stand by the front door. With no invitation, she slipped off her raincoat, hung it on the nearby clothes tree, then headed for the living room. Sitting carefully on the well-worn couch, she hand-pressed a wrinkle out of her pale blue slacks.

Tabby studied her sister. It must be nice to have her good looks, great taste in clothes, and a bubbling personality besides. Compared to Lois's long, carefully curled, silky tresses, Tabby knew her own drab brown, shoulder-length hair must look a mess.

"So, where's your roommate?" Lois asked. "On a rainy day like this, I figured the two of you would probably be curled up on the couch watching one of your favorite boring videos."

"Donna w–went to S–Seattle with her f–folks, and *L–Little W–Women* is not b–boring." Tabby glanced at the video, lying on top of the TV, then she flopped into the rocking chair directly across from her sister. "The b–book is a c–c–classic, and s–s–so is the m–movie."

"Yeah, yeah, I know—little perfect women find their perfect happiness, even though they're poor as scrawny little church mice." Lois sniffed, as though some foul odor had suddenly permeated the room. "The only part of that corny movie I can even relate to is where Jo finally finds her perfect man."

"You've f–found the p–p–perfect man?" Tabby echoed.

Lois nodded. "Definitely. Only mine's not poor. Mike is loaded to the gills, and I'm about to hit pay dirt." She leaned forward, stuck out her left hand, and wiggled her ring finger in front of Tabby's face.

"Wow, w–what a r–r–rock! Does th–this m–m–mean what I th–th–think?"

"It sure as tootin' does, big sister! Mike popped the all important question last night, right in the middle of a romantic candlelight dinner at Roberto's Restaurant." Lois leaned her head against the back of the couch and sighed deeply. "Six months from now, I'll be Mrs. Michael G. Yehley, lady of leisure. No more humdrum life as a small potato's secretary. I plan to spend the rest of my days shopping 'til I drop."

"You're g–getting m–married that s–soon?"

"Don't look so surprised, Shabby Tabby." Lois squinted her eyes. "And for crying out loud, stop that stupid stuttering!"

"I–I–c–can't h–h–help it." Tabby hung her head. "I d–don't d–do it on p–purpose, you—you know."

"Give me a break! You could control it and get over your backward bashfulness if you really wanted to. I think you just do it for attention." Lois pursed her lips. "Your little ploy has never worked on me, though. I would think you'd know that by now."

"I d–do not d–do it for a–attention." Tabby stood up and moved slowly toward the window, a wisp of her sister's expensive perfume filling her nostrils. She grimaced and clasped her trembling hands tightly together. *Now I know I should have gone to Seattle. Even a thousand people closing in around me would have been easier to take than five minutes alone with Lois the Lioness.*

"Are you going to congratulate me or not?"

Tabby forced herself to turn and face her sister again. Lois was tapping her perfectly manicured, long red fingernails along the arm of the couch. "Well?"

"C–c–congratulations," Tabby mumbled.

"C–c–congratulations? Is that all you've got to say?"

"Wh–wh—what else is th–there to s–say?"

"How about, 'I'm very happy for you, Lois?' Or, 'Wow, Sis, I sure wish it were me getting married. Especially since I'm six years older and quickly turning into a dried-up, mousy old maid.' "

Lois's cutting words sliced through Tabby's heart, and a well of emotion rose in her chest, like Mount Saint Helens about to explode. How could anyone be so cruel? So unfeeling? She wished now she had never opened the front door. This visit from her sister wasn't going any better than the last one had. Blinking back unwanted tears, Tabby tried to think of an appropriate comeback.

"Say something. Has the cat grabbed your tongue again?" Lois prompted.

Tabby shrugged. "I–I th–think you'd better just g–g–go."

Her sister stood up quickly, knocking one of the sofa pillows to the floor. "Fine then! Be that way, you little wimp! I'm sorry I even bothered to stop by and share my good news." She swooped her raincoat off the clothes tree, grabbed the umbrella with a snap of her wrist, and stormed out the front door without so much as a backward glance.

Tabby stood staring at the door. "My little sister doesn't think I'll ever amount to anything," she muttered. "Why does she treat me that way?"

Lois is not a Christian, a small voice reminded.

Tabby shuddered. Why was it that whenever she felt sorry for herself, the Lord always came along and gave her a nudge? Tabby's parents weren't churchgoers, either. In fact, they had never understood why, even as a child, Tabby had gotten herself up every Sunday morning and walked to the church two blocks from home. Without Jesus' hand to hold, and the encouragement she got from Donna, she doubted if she would even be working at the day care center.

With a determination she didn't really feel, Tabby squared her shoulders and lifted her chin. "I'll show Lois. I'll show everyone." But even as the words poured out of her mouth, she wondered if it was an impossible dream. What could she, Timid Tabitha, do that would prove to her family that she really was a woman of worth?

two

"I still can't believe I let you talk me into this," Tabby groaned as she settled herself into the passenger seat of Donna's little red car.

Donna put the key in the ignition, then reached over to give Tabby's arm a reassuring squeeze. "It's gonna be fine. Just allow yourself to relax and have a good time. That's what today is all about, you know."

A frown twisted Tabby's lips. "That's easy enough for you to say. You're always so laid back about everything."

"Not always. Remember that blind date my cousin Tom fixed me up with last month? I was a nervous wreck from the beginning to the end of that horrendous evening."

Tabby laughed. "Come on now. It couldn't have been all that bad."

"Oh, yeah?" Donna countered as she pulled out into traffic. "How would you have felt if the most gorgeous guy you'd ever met took you on a bowling date, only because your matchmaking cousin set it all up? I didn't mention it before, but the conceited creep never said more than three words to me all night."

Tabby shrugged. "That would never happen to me, because I'm not about to go on any blind dates. Besides, have you thought maybe the poor guy was just shy? It could be that he wasn't able to conjure up more than three words."

Donna gave the steering wheel a slap with the palm of her hand. "Humph! Rod Thompson was anything but shy. In fact, he spent most of the evening flirting with Carol, my cousin's date."

14

Tabby squinted her eyes. "You're kidding."

"I'm not. It was probably the worst night of my life." Donna wiggled her eyebrows. "It was nearly enough to throw me straight into the arms of our preacher's son."

"Alex? Has Alex asked you out?"

"Many times, and my answer is always no."

"Why? Alex Hanson is cute."

Donna released a low moan. "I know, but he's a PK, for crying out loud! Nobody in their right mind wants to date a preacher's kid."

Tabby's forehead wrinkled, and she pushed a lock of hair away from her face. "Why not? What's wrong with a preacher's kid?"

Donna laughed. "Haven't you heard? The pastor and his entire family live in a fish bowl. Everyone expects them to be perfect."

"If Alex is perfect, then what's the big problem?"

"I said, he's supposed to be perfect. Most of the PKs I've ever known are far from perfect."

Tabby chuckled. "I have a feeling you really like Alex."

"I do not!"

"Do so!"

"Do not!"

Their childish banter went on until Tabby finally called a truce by changing the subject. "Which workshop are you going to register for at the seminar?" she asked.

Donna smiled. "Chalk art drawing. I've always been interested in art, and if I can manage to use my meager talent in that form of Christian ministry, then I'm ready, able, and more than willing."

Tabby glanced down at the scruffy little puppet lying in her lap. "I sure hope I won't have to talk to anyone. Unless I'm behind a puppet box, that is." She slipped Roscoe onto her hand. "If I'm well hidden and can talk through this little guy, I might actually learn something today."

"You're just too self-conscious for your own good. You've got such potential, and I hate to see you waste it."

"Potential? You must have me mixed up with someone else."

Donna clicked her tongue. "Would you please stop? You'll never build your confidence or get over being shy if you keep putting yourself down all the time."

"What am I supposed to do? Brag about how cute, smart, and talented I am?" Tabby grimaced. "Take a good look at me, Donna. I'm the plainest Jane around town, and as I've reminded you before, I can barely say two words to anyone but you or the day care kids without stuttering and making a complete fool of myself."

"You want people to accept you, but you don't think you can ever measure up. Am I right?"

Tabby nodded.

"That will all change," Donna insisted. "Just as soon as you realize your full potential. Repeat after me—I can do it. I can do it. I can do it!"

Tabby held Roscoe up and squeaked, "I can do it, but that's just because I'm a dumb little dog."

❧

The foyer of Alliance Community Church was crammed with people. Tabby gulped down a wave of nausea and steadied herself against the sign-up table for the puppet workshop. She was sure that coming here had been a terrible mistake. If not for the fact that Donna was already in line at the chalk art registration table, she might have turned around and bolted for the door.

"Sorry, but this class is filled up," said a soft-spoken older woman behind the puppet registration table.

"It—it—is?" Tabby stammered.

"I'm afraid so. You might try the ventriloquist workshop." The woman motioned toward a table across the room. "If you like puppetry, I'm sure you'd love to try talking for two."

Tabby slipped quietly away from the table, holding Roscoe so tightly her hand ached. There was no more room in the puppet workshop. Now she had a viable excuse to get out of this crowded place. She turned toward the front door and started to run. Pushing her way past several people, she came to a halt when she ran straight into a man.

"Whoa!" his deep voice exclaimed. "What's your hurry?"

Tabby stared up at him in stunned silence. She was rewarded with a wide smile.

Her plan had been to make a hasty exit, but this young man with soft auburn hair and seeking green eyes had blocked her path.

He nodded toward the puppet she was clutching. "Are you signed up for my class?"

Her gaze was drawn to the stark white piece of paper he held in his hand. "I—uh—th—that is—"

"I hope you're not self-conscious about using a hand puppet instead of a dummy. Many ventriloquists use puppets quite effectively."

Tabby gulped and felt the strength drain from her shaky legs. The guy thought she wanted to learn ventriloquism, and apparently he was the teacher for that workshop. The idea of talking for two and learning to throw her voice did have a certain measure of appeal, but could she? Would she have the nerve to sit in a class with people she didn't even know? Could she talk for her puppet without a puppet box to hide behind? *Maybe I could just sit quietly and observe. Maybe I'd never have to say a word.*

&

As she studied the handout sheet she'd just been given, Tabby wondered what on earth had possessed her to take a ventriloquist class, of all things! She felt about as dumb as a box of rocks, but as she pondered the matter, an idea burst into her head. Maybe she could do some short ventriloquist skits for the day care kids. If they liked Roscoe popping up from behind a desk, how much more might they enjoy seeing him out in plain view? If she could speak without moving her lips, the kids would think Roscoe really could talk.

From her seat at the back of the classroom, Tabby let her gaze travel toward the front. The young man with short-cropped auburn hair had just introduced himself as Seth Beyers, owner and operator of Beyers' Ventriloquist Studio. He was holding a full-sized, professional ventriloquist figure with one hand.

"I'd like to give you a little rundown on the background of ventriloquism before we begin," Seth said. "Some history books try to date ventriloquism back to biblical times, citing the story of Saul's visit to the witch of Endor as a basis for their claim." He frowned. "I disagree with this theory, though. As a believer in Christ, I take the scriptural account literally for what it says. In fact, I don't think the Bible makes any reference to ventriloquism at all.

"Ventriloquism is nothing more than an illusion. A ventriloquist talks and creates the impression that a voice is coming from somewhere other than its true source. People are often fooled into believing the ventriloquist is throwing his voice. Ventriloquism has been around a long time. Even the ancient Greeks did it. Romans thought ventriloquists spoke from their stomachs. In fact, the word ventriloquism comes from two Latin roots—*venter*—meaning belly, and *loqui*—the past participle of the verb *locuts*, which means to speak."

Seth smiled. "So, the word ventriloquism is actually a misnomer, for there is really no such thing as stomach talking. A ventriloquist's voice comes from only one place—his own throat. Everything the ventriloquist does and says makes the onlooker believe his voice comes from someplace else."

Positioning his foot on the seat of an empty folding chair,

Seth placed the dummy on top of his knee. "Most of you will probably start by using an inexpensive plastic figure, or even a hand puppet." Gesturing toward the dummy, Seth added, "Later on, as you become more comfortable doing ventriloquism, you might want to purchase a professional figure like my woodenheaded friend, Rudy."

Suddenly it was as though the dummy had jumped to life. "Hi, folks! My name's Rudy Right, and I'm always right!"

A few snickers filtered through the room, and Seth reprimanded his little friend. "No way, Rudy. No one but God is always right."

"Is that so? Well, in the dummy world, I'm always right!" Rudy shot back.

Tabby leaned forward, watching intently. Seth's lips didn't move at all, and the sound supposedly coming from Rudy Right was nothing like the instructor's deep voice. If common sense hadn't taken over, she might have actually believed the dummy could talk. *A child would surely believe it. Kids probably relate well to what the dummy says too.*

Yanking her wayward thoughts back to the happenings at the front of the room, Tabby giggled behind her hand when Rudy Right accused his owner of being a bigger dummy than he was.

"Yep," spouted Rudy, "you'd have to be really dumb to wanna be around dummies all the time." With the wink of one doeskin eye, the woodenhead added, "Maybe I should start pullin' your strings and see how you like it!"

When the laughter died down, Seth made Rudy say goodbye, then promptly put him back in the suitcase from which he'd first appeared. With a muffled voice from inside the case, Rudy hollered, "Hey, who turned out the lights?"

In the moment of enjoyment, Tabby laughed out loud, temporarily forgetting her uncomfortable shyness. Everyone clapped, and the expert ventriloquist took a bow.

"I see a few of you have brought along a puppet or dummy this morning," Seth said. "So, who would like to be the first to come up and try saying the easy alphabet with the use of your ventriloquist partner?"

When no one volunteered, Seth pointed right at Tabby. "How about you, there in the back row?"

Her heart fluttered like a bird's wings. She bit her bottom lip, then ducked her head, wanting to speak but afraid to do so.

Seth took a few steps toward her. "I'm referring to the young woman with the cute little dog puppet."

If there had only been a hole in the floor, Tabby would have crawled straight into it. She felt trapped, like a caged animal at the Point Defiance Zoo. She wanted to tell Seth Beyers that she wasn't ready to try the easy alphabet yet. However, she knew what would happen if she even tried to speak. Everything would come out in a jumble of incoherent, stuttering words, and she'd be completely mortified. Slinking down in her chair, face red as a vine-ripened tomato, she merely shook her head.

"I guess the little lady's not quite up to the task yet," Seth responded with a chuckle. "Is there someone else brave enough to let us critique you?"

One hand from the front row shot up. Seth nodded. "Okay, you're on!"

An attractive young woman with long red hair took her place next to Seth. She was holding a small boy dummy and wearing a smile that stretched from ear to ear. "Hi, my name's Cheryl Stone, and this is my friend, Oscar."

"Have you done any ventriloquism before?" Seth questioned.

Cheryl snickered. "Just in front of my bedroom mirror. I've read a book about throwing your voice, but I haven't mastered all the techniques yet."

"Then you have a bit of an advantage." Seth flashed her a reassuring smile.

Tabby felt a surge of envy course through her veins. Here were two good-looking redheads, standing in front of an audience with their dummies, and neither one looked the least bit nervous. Why in the world did she have to be so paralyzed with fear? What kept her locked in the confines of "Timid Tabitha"?

"Okay, let's begin with that easy alphabet," Seth said, breaking into Tabby's troubling thoughts. "All the letters printed on the blackboard can be said without moving your lips. I'll point to each one, and Cheryl will have her dummy repeat after me."

Cheryl nodded. "We're ready when you are."

Seth moved toward the portable blackboard positioned at Cheryl's left. "Don't forget to keep your mouth relaxed and slightly open, biting your top teeth lightly down on the bottom teeth." Using a pointer-stick, Seth began to call out the letters of the easy alphabet.

Cheryl made Oscar repeat each one. "A C D E G H I J K L N O Q R S T U X Y Z."

She'd done it almost perfectly, and Seth smiled in response. "Sometimes the letter Y can be a problem, but it's easy enough if you just say ooh-eye."

"What about the other letters in the alphabet?" an older man in the audience asked. "What are we supposed to do when we say a word that has B, F, M, P, V, or W in it?"

"That's a good question," Seth replied. "Those all get sound substitutions, and we'll be dealing with that problem shortly."

Oh, no, Tabby groaned inwardly. *This class is going to be anything but easy.*

"Let's have Cheryl and her little friend read some sentences for us," Seth continued. Below the easy alphabet letters he wrote a few lines. "Okay, have a go at it."

"Yes, I can do it." Cheryl opened and closed her dummy's mouth in perfect lip sync. "She had a red silk hat, and that is no joke!"

Everyone laughed, and Cheryl took a bow.

Seth erased the words, then wrote a few more sentences. "Now try these."

"I ran across the yard, heading to the zoo. I need to get a key and unlock the car."

Tabby wrestled with her feelings of jealousy as Cheryl stood there looking so confident and saying everything with no lip movement at all. Tabby sucked in her bottom lip and tried to concentrate on learning the easy alphabet. After all, it wasn't Cheryl's fault she was talented and Tabby wasn't.

"That was great, Cheryl!" Seth gave her a pat on the back.

She smiled in response. "Thanks. It was fun."

The next few hours flew by, with only one fifteen-minute break for snacks and use of the restrooms. Tabby's plan had been to sneak out during this time and wait for Donna in the car. The whole concept of ventriloquism had her fascinated, though, and even if she wasn't going to actively participate, she knew she simply couldn't leave now.

By the time the class finally wound down, everyone had been given a video tape, an audiocassette, and several handouts. Everything from the easy alphabet to proper breathing and sound substitutions had been covered. Now all Tabby had to do was go home and practice. Only then would she know if she could ever learn to talk for two.

three

"You're awfully quiet," Donna said, as they began their drive home from the seminar. "Didn't you enjoy the puppet workshop?"

"I never went," Tabby replied.

"Never went?"

"Nope. The class was filled up."

"If you didn't go to the workshop, then where have you been all morning, and why are you holding a bunch of hand-outs and tapes?"

"I was learning ventriloquism."

Donna's dark eyebrows shot up. "Ventriloquism? You mean you took the workshop on how to throw your voice?"

"Yeah, and I think I threw mine away for good."

"It went that badly, huh?"

Tabby's only reply was a slow sweep of her hand.

"What on earth possessed you to take something as difficult as ventriloquism?" Donna questioned. "I'm the adventuresome type, and I'd never try anything like that."

Tabby crossed her arms. "Beats me."

"Did you learn anything?"

"I learned that in order to talk for two, I'd need talent and nerves of steel." Tabby groaned. "Neither of which I happen to have."

Donna gave the steering wheel a light rap with her knuckles. "Tabitha Johnson, will you please quit putting yourself down? You've got plenty of talent. You just need to begin utilizing it."

"You didn't say anything about nerves of steel, though," Tabby reminded. "Being shy is definitely my worst shortcoming, and without self-confidence, I could never be a ventriloquist."

"I wouldn't be so sure about that."

"Right! Can't you just see it? Timid Tabitha shuffles on stage, takes one look at the audience, and closes up like a razor clam." She wrinkled her nose. "Or worse yet, I'd start to speak, then get so tongue-tied every word would come out in a jumble of uncontrollable stuttering."

Donna seemed to be mulling things over. "Hmm. . ."

"Hmm. . .what?"

"Why don't you practice your ventriloquism skills on me, then put on a little program for the day care kids?"

"I've already thought about that. It's probably the only way I could ever talk for two." Tabby shrugged. "Who knows—it might even be kind of fun."

"Now that's the spirit! I think we should stop by the Burger Barn and celebrate."

"You call that a place of celebration?"

Donna laughed. "Sure, if you love the triple-decker cheeseburger—and I do!"

Tabby slipped Roscoe onto her hand. "Okay, girls, Burger Barn, here we come!"

&

In spite of the fact that he'd lost a whole morning of work, Seth had actually enjoyed teaching the ventriloquism workshop. With the exception of that one extremely shy young woman, it had been exciting to see how many in the class caught on so quickly. The little gal holding a scruffy dog puppet had remained in the back row, scrunched down in her seat, looking like she was afraid of her own shadow. She never participated in any way.

Seth had encountered a few bashful people over the years, but no one seemed as self-restricted as that poor woman. Whenever he tried to make eye contact or ask her a question, she seemed to freeze. After a few tries he'd finally given up, afraid she might bolt for the door and miss the whole workshop.

A muscle twitched in his jaw. *I really wish I could have gotten through somehow. What was the point in her taking the class, if she wasn't going to join in? But then, who knows, the shy one might actually take the tapes and handouts home, practice like crazy, and become the next Shari Lewis.*

He chuckled out loud. "Naw, that might be stretching things a bit."

Gathering up his notes, Seth grabbed Rudy's suitcase. He needed to get back to the shop and resume work on Alan Capshaw's ugly dummy. There would be another full day tomorrow, since he was going to be part of a Christian workers' demonstration at a church in the north end of Tacoma.

Seth didn't get to worship at his home church much anymore. He was frequently asked to do programs for other churches' Sunday schools, junior church, or special services that might help generate more interest in Christian ministry. Between that and his full-time business, there wasn't much time left for socializing. Seth hoped that would all change some day. Not that he planned to quit serving the Lord with the talents he'd been generously given. No, as long as the opportunity arose, he would try to follow God's leading and remain faithfully in His service.

What Seth really wanted to modify was his social life. Keeping company with a bunch of dummies was not all that stimulating, and even performing for large crowds wasn't the same as a meaningful one-on-one conversation with someone who shared his interests and love for God.

"Well, Rudy Right," Seth said, glancing at the suitcase in his hand, "I guess it's just you and me for the rest of the day."

❧

The Burger Barn was crowded. Hoping to avoid the mass of people, Tabby suggested they use the drive-thru.

"Part of the fun of going in is being able to check out all the good-looking guys," Donna argued.

Tabby wrinkled her nose. "You do the checking out, and I'll just eat."

A short time later, they were munching their food and discussing the workshop.

"Tell me about the chalk art class," Tabby said. "Did you learn anything helpful?"

Donna's face lit up. "It was wonderful! In fact, I think I'm gonna try my hand at black light."

"Black light?"

"You hook a thin, black light over the top of your easel. The pictures you draw with fluorescent chalk almost come to life." Donna motioned with her hand, as though she were drawing an imaginary illustration. "I wish you could have seen some of the beautiful compositions our instructor put together. She draws well anyway, but under the black light, her pictures were absolutely gorgeous!"

Tabby smiled. "I can see she really inspired you to use your artistic talent."

"I'll say. I thought maybe you and I could combine our talents and put on a little program during Sunday school opening sometime."

"You're kidding, right?"

"I'm not kidding at all. I could do a chalk art drawing, and you could put on a puppet show. You might be able to use that old puppet box down in the church storage room." Donna gulped down her lemonade and rushed on. "It's not like you'd have to try your new ventriloquist skills or anything. You could hide behind the puppet box, and—"

Tabby held up one hand. "Whoa! In the first place, I have no ventriloquist skills. Furthermore, I've never done puppets anywhere but at the day care. I'm not sure I could ever do anything for church."

"Sure you could," Donna insisted. "Tomorrow, during our morning worship service, we're going to be entertained and inspired by some of the best Christian education workers in the Puget Sound area."

Tabby's interest was piqued. "We are? I hadn't heard. Guess I've been spending too much time helping out in the church nursery lately."

Donna smiled. "There will be a puppet team from Edmonds, Washington, a chalk artist from Seattle, a ventriloquist, who I hear is a local guy, and several others."

Tabby stared out the window. *Hmm. . .seeing some professionals perform might be kind of interesting. No way does it mean I'll agree to Donna's harebrained idea of us performing at Sunday school, though. I'll just find a seat in the back row and simply enjoy the show.*

⊷

The church service would be starting soon, and Seth hurried through the hall toward the sanctuary. Someone had just come out of the ladies' restroom, head down and feet shuffling in his direction. Thump! She bumped straight into his arm, nearly knocking little Rudy to the floor.

From the startled expression on her face, Seth could tell she was just as surprised to see him as he was to see her. "Oh, excuse me!" he apologized.

"It's–it's o–o–okay," the young woman stammered. "It w–w–was probably m–m–my fault."

Seth smiled, trying to put her at ease. "I was the instructor at the ventriloquism workshop you took yesterday; do you remember?"

She hung her head and mumbled, "Y–y–yes, I kn–kn–know who y–y–you are. S–s–sorry for g–g–getting in the w–way."

"Naw, it was all my owner's fault," Seth made his dummy say in a high-pitched voice. "He's got two left feet, and I guess he wasn't watchin' where he was goin'." The vent figure gave her a quick wink, then added, "My name's Rudy Right, and I'm always right. What's your name, Sister?"

"My name's Tabitha Johnson, but you can call me Tabby." She reached out to grasp one of the dummy's small wooden hands.

Seth grinned. By talking to her through his partner, Tabby seemed much more relaxed. She was even able to make eye contact—at least with the dummy. *I should have tried that in the workshop yesterday. She might have been a bit more receptive.*

Seth had used his ventriloquist figure to reach frightened, sick, and even a few autistic children on more than one occasion. They had always been able to relate better to the dummy than they had to him, so maybe the concept would work as well on adults who had a problem with shyness. He also remembered recently reading an article on stuttering, which seemed to be Tabby's problem. One of the most important things a person could do when talking to someone who stuttered was to be patient and listen well. He thought he could do both, so Seth decided to try a little experiment. "It was nice having you in my workshop," he said, speaking for himself this time.

Tabby's gaze dropped immediately to the floor. "It w–w–was good."

"Did ya learn anything?" This question came from Rudy.

Tabby nodded, looking right at the dummy, whose eyes were now flitting from side to side.

"What'd ya learn?" Rudy prompted.

"I learned that ventriloquism is not as easy as it looks."

No stuttering at all this time, Seth noted. *Hmm. . .I think I may be on to something here.*

"Are you gonna be a ven-trick-o-list?" Rudy asked, giving Tabby a wink.

Tabby giggled. "I'd like to be, but I'm not sure I'd have the nerve to stand up in front of people and talk."

"Aw, it's a piece of cake," Rudy drawled. "All ya have to do is smile, grit your teeth, and let your dummy do most of the talkin'." The figure's head cranked to the left. "Of course, ya need to find a better lookin' dummy than the one I got stuck with!"

At this, Rudy began to howl, and Tabby laughed right along with him.

Seth's experiment had worked, and he felt as if he'd just climbed to the summit of Mount Rainier.

"I'm surprised to see you here today," Tabby said, directing her comment at Rudy.

The dummy's head swiveled, and his blue eyes rolled back and forth again. "My dummy was asked to give a little demonstration during your worship time. I just came along to keep him in line."

"And to be sure I don't flirt with all the cute women," Seth added in his own voice.

Tabby's face flushed. "I—uh—it's been n–nice t–t–talking to you. I th–think I sh–should g–go find a s–seat in the s–s–sanctuary now."

"Maybe I'll see you later," Seth called to her retreating form.

 та

Tabby slid into a back-row pew, next to Donna.

"What took you so long? I thought I might have to send out the Coast Guard, just in case you'd fallen overboard or something."

Tabby groaned at Donna's tasteless comment. "I ran into the ventriloquist who taught the workshop I took yesterday."

"You did? What's he doing here?"

"He's part of the demonstration. He brought along his cute little dummy."

"I guess he would, if he's going to do ventriloquism." Donna sent a quick jab to Tabby's ribs with her elbow. "Did he talk to you?"

"Who?"

Another jab to the ribs. "The ventriloquist, of course."

"Actually, it was the dummy who did most of the talking. He was so funny too."

Donna nodded. "I guess in order to be a ventriloquist, you'd need a good sense of humor."

Tabby twisted her hands together in her lap. How in the world did she think she could ever talk for two? Humor and wisecracking didn't come easy for someone like her. She was about to relay that to Donna, but the church service had begun. She turned her full attention to the front of the room instead.

Mr. Hartung, the middle-aged song leader, led the congregation in several praise choruses, followed by a few hymns. Announcements were given next, then the offering was taken. After that, Pastor Smith encouraged the congregation to use their talents to serve the Lord, and he introduced the group who had come to inspire others to use their talents in the area of Christian ministry.

The first to perform was Mark Taylor, a Christian magician from Portland, Oregon. He did a few sleight-of-hand tricks, showing how sin can seriously affect one's life. Using another illusion, he showed the way to be shed of sin, through Jesus Christ.

Next up was Gail Stevens, a chalk artist from Seattle. She amazed the congregation with her beautiful chalk drawing of Christ's ascension into heaven, adding a special touch by using the black light Donna had been so enthusiastic about. This illuminated the entire picture and seemed to bring the illustration to life, as Jesus rose in a vibrant, fluorescent, pink cloud.

There were oohs and ahs all around the room, and Donna nudged Tabby again. "That's what I want to be able to do someday."

Tabby nodded. "I'm sure you will too."

A group of puppeteers put on a short musical routine, using several Muppet-style puppets, who sang to a taped version of "Bullfrogs and Butterflies." Tabby enjoyed their skit but was most anxious for the upcoming ventriloquist routine.

Joe Richey, a gospel clown from Olympia, did a short pantomime, which he followed with a demonstration on balloon sculpting. He made a simple dog with a long body, a colorful bouquet of flowers, and ended the routine by making a seal balancing a ball on the end of its nose. Everyone clapped as Slow-Joe the Clown handed out his balloon creations to several excited children in the audience.

Seth Beyers finally took his place in the center of the platform.

"There he is," Tabby whispered breathlessly. "And that's his cute little dummy, Rudy."

Seth had already begun to speak, and Tabby chose to ignore her friend when she asked, "Who do you really think is cute? The funny-looking dummy or the good-looking guy who's pulling his strings?"

"I would like you all to meet my little buddy, Rudy," Seth boomed into the microphone.

"That's right—I'm Rudy Right, and I'm always right!"

"Now, Rudy, I've told you many times that no one but God is always right."

Rudy's glass eyes moved from side to side. "Is that so? I guess we must be related then!"

"The Bible says that God made people in His own image, and you're certainly not a person."

There was a long pause, as if Rudy might be mulling over what the ventriloquist had said. Finally, the dummy's mouth dropped open. "I may be just a dummy, but I'm smart enough to pull your strings!"

Seth laughed, and so did the audience.

Donna leaned close to Tabby, "This guy's really good. His

lips don't move at all."

Tabby smiled. "I know." Oh, how she wished she could perform like that, without stuttering or passing out from stage fright. What a wonderful way ventriloquism was to teach Bible stories and the important lessons of life.

A troubling thought popped into Tabby's head, pushing aside her excitement over the ventriloquism routine. *What would it feel like to have someone as good-looking, talented, and friendly as Seth Beyers be interested in someone as dull and uninteresting as me?*

four

"Wasn't that program great?" Donna asked, as she steered her car out of the church parking lot. "Could you believe how gorgeous the chalk art picture was under the black light?"

"Uh-huh," Tabby mumbled.

"And did you see how quickly Gail Stevens drew that picture? If I drew even half that fast, I'd probably end up with more chalk on me than the paper."

"Hmm. . ."

Donna glanced Tabby's way. "Is that all you've got to say? What's wrong with you, anyway? Ever since we walked out the door, you've been acting like you're a million miles away."

Tabby merely shrugged her shoulders in reply.

"Since my folks are out of town this weekend, and Mom won't be cooking us her usual Sunday dinner, should we eat out or fend for ourselves at home?"

Tabby shrugged again. "Whatever you think. I'm not all that hungry anyway."

"What? Tabitha Johnson not hungry?" Donna raised her eyebrows. "Surely you jest!"

Tucking a thumbnail between her teeth, Tabby mumbled, "I've never been much into 'jesting.' "

Donna reached across the short span of her car to give Tabby's arm a quick jab. "I've seen the little puppet skits you put on for the kids at our day care. I think they're quite humorous, and so do the children."

Tabby felt her jaw tense. "You're just saying that to make me feel better."

"Uh-uh, I really do think your puppet routines are funny."

33

"That's because I'm well out of sight, and only the silly-looking dog is in the limelight." Tabby grimaced. "If I had to stand up in front of an audience the way Seth Beyers did today, I think I'd curl up and die right on the spot."

"You know, Tabby, ventriloquism might be the very thing to help you overcome your shyness."

"How can you say that, Donna? I'd have to talk in front of people."

"Yes, but you'd be talking through your dummy."

"Dummy? What dummy? I don't even have a dummy?"

"I know, but you could get one."

"In case you haven't heard—those lifelike things are really expensive. Besides, I'm only going to be doing ventriloquism for the kids at day care. Roscoe's good enough for that." She inhaled deeply. "Of course I have to start practicing first, and only time will tell whether I can actually learn to talk for two.

ð

As Seth Beyers drove home from church, a keen sense of disappointment flooded his soul. The realization that he hadn't seen Tabby Johnson after the morning service didn't hit him until now.

During his little performance with Rudy, he'd spotted her sitting in the very back row. After the service he had been swarmed by people full of questions about ventriloquism and asking for all kinds of information about the dummies he created and repaired.

Tabby had obviously slipped out the door while he'd been occupied. He would probably never see her again. For reasons beyond his comprehension, that thought made him sad.

He reflected on something Grandpa had recently told him: "Everyone needs to feel as if they count for something, Seth. If you recognize that need in dealing with people, you might be able to help someone learn to like themselves a bit more."

Seth knew his grandfather's advice was good, and as much

as he'd like to help Tabby, he also knew all he could really do was pray for the introverted young woman. He promised himself he would remember to do so.

ж

Tabby had been practicing ventriloquism for several weeks. She'd often sit in front of the full-length mirror in her bedroom, completely alone except for Roscoe Puppet. Not even Donna had been allowed to see her struggle through those first few difficult attempts at talking for two. If Tabby were ever going to perform for the day care kids, it wouldn't be until she had complete control of her lip movement and had perfected those horrible sound substitutions. There was *th* for v and f, *d* for b, and *n* for m. It was anything but easy, and it was enough to make her crazy!

Tabby took a seat in front of the mirror, slipped Roscoe onto her hand, and held him next to her face. "What do you think, little buddy? Can we ever learn to do ventriloquism well enough to put on a short skit for the kids?"

Manipulating the puppet's mouth, she made him say, "I think we can. . . I think we can. . . I think I have a bang-up plan. You throw your voice, and let me say all the funny stuff."

Tabby smiled triumphantly. "I did it! I said the sound substitutions without any lip movement!" She jumped to her feet, jerked open the door, and bolted into the living room. Donna was there, working on a chalk drawing taped to her easel. Tabby held Roscoe in front of her face. "I think I'm finally getting the hang of it!"

Donna kept on drawing. "The hang of what?"

Tabby dropped to the couch with a groan. "I'm trying to tell you that I can talk without moving my lips."

Donna finally set her work aside and turned to face Tabby. "That's great. How about a little demonstration?"

Tabby swallowed hard, and a few tears rolled unexpectedly down her cheeks.

Donna was at her side immediately. "What's wrong? I

thought you'd be thrilled about your new talent."

"I am, but I wonder if I'll ever have the nerve to actually use it." She swiped at the tears and sniffed. "I really do want to serve God using ventriloquism, but it seems so hard."

"God never promised that serving Him in any way would be easy," Donna said. "And may I remind you of the acts you already do to serve the Lord?"

Tabby sucked in her bottom lip. "Like what?"

"You teach the day care kids about Jesus. You bake cookies for the residents of Rose Park Convalescent Center. You also read your Bible, pray, and—"

Tabby held up one hand. "Okay, okay. . .I get the picture. What I want to know is, are you saying I should be content to serve God in those ways and forget all about ventriloquism?"

Donna shook her head. "No, of course not. You just need to keep on trying and never give up. I believe God wants all Christians to use their talents and serve Him through whatever means they can."

Running a hand through her hair, Tabby nodded. "All right. I'll try."

With fear and trembling, Tabby forced herself to do a short ventriloquist routine the following day for the day care kids. Fifteen little ones sat cross-legged on the carpeted floor, looking up at her expectantly.

Tabby put Roscoe on one hand, and in the other hand she held a small bag of dog food. Drawing in a deep breath, she began. "R–R–Roscoe wants to tell you a little st–st–story today."

Tabby couldn't believe she was stuttering. She never stuttered in front of the kids. *It's only my nerves. They'll settle down in a few minutes.*

Several children clapped, and one little freckle-faced, redheaded boy called out, "Go, Roscoe! Go!"

Tabby gulped. It was now or never.

"Hey, kids—what's up?" the puppet said in a gravely voice.

So far so good. No lip movement, and Roscoe's lip sync was right on.

"We just had lunch," a young girl shouted.

Tabby chuckled, feeling herself beginning to relax. "That's right," she said to the puppet. "The kids had macaroni and cheese today."

Pointing Roscoe's nose in the air, Tabby made him say, "I think I smell somethin' else."

"They had hot dogs too. That's probably what you smell."

"Hot dogs? They had hot dogs?"

Tabby nodded. "That's right, now it's time for your lunch."

"Oh, boy! I get a nice, big, juicy hot dog!"

"No, I have your favorite kind of dog food." Tabby held the bag high in the air.

Roscoe's furry head shook from side to side. "No way! I hate dog food! It's for dogs!"

The children laughed, and Donna, standing at the back of the room, gave Tabby an approving nod.

Tabby's enthusiasm began to soar as she plunged ahead. "But, Roscoe, you are a dog. Dogs are supposed to eat dog food, not people food."

"That's easy for you to say," Roscoe croaked. "Have you ever chomped down on a stale piece of dry old dog food?"

"I can't say as I have."

"Dog food makes me sick," Roscoe whined.

"I never knew that."

Roscoe's head bobbed up and down. "It's the truth. In fact, I was so sick the other day, I had to go to the vet."

"Really?"

"Yep! The vet took my temperature and everything."

"What'd he say?" Tabby prompted.

"He said, 'Hot dog!' " The puppet's head tipped back, and he let out a high-pitched howl.

By the time Tabby was done with her routine, Donna was laughing so hard she had tears rolling down her cheeks. As soon as the children went down for their afternoon naps, she took Tabby aside. "That was great. You're really good at talking for two."

"You think so?"

"Yes, I do. Not only have you mastered lip control and sound substitutions, but your routine was hilarious. Where did you come up with all those cute lines?"

Tabby shrugged. "Beats me. I just kind of ad-libbed as I went along."

Donna gave Tabby a quick hug. "Now all you need is a good ventriloquist dummy."

With an exasperated groan, Tabby dropped into one of the kiddy chairs. "Let's not get into that again. I can't afford one of those professional figures, and since I'll only be performing here at the day care, Roscoe will work just fine!"

❧

Seth was nearly finished with the ugly dummy he was making for Alan Capshaw. While it had turned out well enough, it wasn't to his personal liking. A good ventriloquist didn't need an ugly dummy in order to captivate an audience. A professional ventriloquist needed talent, humor, and a purpose. For Seth, that purpose was sharing the gospel and helping others find a meaningful relationship with Christ.

In deep concentration at his workbench, Seth didn't even hear the overhead bell ring when a customer entered his shop. Not until he smelled the faint lilac scent of a woman's perfume and heard a polite, "Ah-hem," did he finally look up from his work.

A young, attractive woman with short, dark curls stood on the other side of the long wooden counter.

Seth placed the ugly dummy aside and skirted quickly around his workbench. "May I help you?"

"Yes. I was wondering if you have gift certificates for the dummies you sell."

Seth smiled. "Sure. For what value did you want it?"

"Would three hundred dollars buy a fairly nice dummy?"

He nodded. "Prices for ventriloquist figures range any-where from one hundred dollars for a small, inexpensive model to seven hundred dollars for one with all the extras.

"I'd like a gift certificate for three hundred dollars then."

Seth went to his desk, retrieved the gift certificate book, accepted the young woman's check, and in short order, the business was concluded.

"Are you a ventriloquist?" he asked when she put the certificate in her purse and started to turn away.

She hesitated, then pivoted to face him. "No, but a friend of mine is, and she's got a birthday coming up soon."

"You're giving her a professional figure?"

"Sort of. She'll actually be the one forced to come in here and pick it up."

"Forced?" Seth's eyebrows arched upwards. "Why would anyone have to be forced to cash in a gift certificate for a ventriloquist dummy?"

"My friend is extremely shy," the woman explained. "It's hard for her to talk to people."

"Your friend's name wouldn't happen to be Tabby Johnson, would it?"

"How did you know that?"

"I thought I recognized you when you first came in. Now I know from where." Seth extended his right hand. "I'm Seth Beyers. I saw Tabby sitting with you during the Christian workers' program at your church a few weeks ago."

"I'm Donna Hartley, and Tabby and I have been friends since we were kids. She said she spoke with you. Well, actu-ally, I guess it was more to your dummy."

Seth nodded. "I could hardly get her to make eye contact."

"That's not surprising."

"Whenever she talked to me, she stuttered." His forehead wrinkled. "She could talk a blue streak to my little pal, Rudy, and never miss a syllable."

Donna shrugged. "To be perfectly honest, besides me, the day care kids are the only ones she can talk to without stuttering."

"Day care kids?"

"Our church has a day care center, and Tabby and I manage it. It's about the only kind of work Tabby can do. Her self-esteem is really low, and I seriously doubt she'd ever make it around adults all day."

Seth couldn't begin to imagine how Tabby must feel. He usually didn't suffer from low self-esteem—unless you could count the fact that he hadn't found the right woman yet. Occasionally he found himself wondering if he had some kind of personality defect.

"Do you think ventriloquism might help Tabby?" Donna asked, breaking into his thoughts.

He shrugged. "Maybe."

"Tabby did a short routine at the day care the other day. It went really well, and I think it gave her a bit more confidence."

Seth scratched the back of his head. He felt like taking on a new challenge. "Hmm. . . Maybe we could work on this problem together."

Donna's eyebrows furrowed. "What do you mean?"

"You keep encouraging her to perform more, and when she comes in to pick out her new dummy, I'll try to work on her from this end."

Donna's expression revealed her obvious surprise. "You'd do that for a complete stranger?"

" 'Whatever you did for one of the least of these brothers of mine, you did for me,' " Seth quoted from the Book of Matthew.

"I like your Christian attitude," Donna said as she turned to leave. "Thanks for everything." After the door closed behind her, Seth let out a piercing whoop. He would soon be seeing Tabby again. Maybe he could actually help her. Maybe this was the answer to his prayers.

five

"I wish you weren't making such a big deal over my birthday," Tabby grumbled as she and Donna drove home from the grocery store one evening after work. This time they were in Tabby's blue hatchback, and she was in the driver's seat.

"It's just gonna be a barbecue in my parents' backyard," Donna argued. "How can that be labeled a big deal?"

Tabby grimaced. "You ordered a fancy cake, bought three flavors of ice cream, and invited half the city of Tacoma!"

"Oh, please! Your folks, Lois, her boyfriend, your grandma, me, and my folks—that's half of Tacoma?" Donna poked Tabby on the arm. "Besides, your folks live in Olympia now."

"I know, but being with my family more than twenty minutes makes me feel like it's half of Tacoma," Tabby argued.

"It isn't every day that my best friend turns twenty-five," Donna persisted. "If I want to throw her a big party, then it's my right to do so."

"I don't mean to sound ungrateful, but you know how things are between me and my family," Tabby reminded.

Donna nodded. "Yes, I do, and I know your parents often hurt you by the unkind things they say and do, but you can't pull away from them and stay in your cocoon of shyness. You don't have to like what they say and do, but you've got to love your family anyway." She sighed. "What I'm trying to say is, you've gotta love 'em, but you can't let them run your life or destroy your confidence, the way you've been doing for so long. It's high time for you to stand up and be counted."

"Yeah, right. Like that could ever happen."

41

"It could if you gained some self-confidence and quit letting Lois overshadow you."

"Fat chance! Just wait 'til you see the size of her engagement ring. It looks like Mount Rainier!"

Donna laughed. "How you do exaggerate."

"She's only marrying this guy for his money. Did I tell you that?"

"Only about a hundred times."

"I think it's disgusting." Tabby frowned. "I'd never marry anyone unless I loved him. Of course, he'd have to be a Christian," she quickly added.

"I'm beginning to think neither of us will ever find a husband," Donna said. "You're too shy, and I'm too picky."

"I can't argue with that. Unless I find a man who's either just a big kid or a real dummy, I'd never be able to talk to him."

"Maybe you can find a ventriloquist to marry, then let your dummies do all the talking."

Tabby groaned. "Now there's a brilliant idea. I can see it now—me, walking down the aisle, carrying a dummy instead of a bouquet. My groom would be waiting at the altar, holding his own dummy, of course."

Donna chuckled. "You are so funny today. Too bad the rest of the world can't see the real Tabitha Johnson."

≈

The birthday party was set to begin at six o'clock on Saturday night, in the backyard of Donna's parents, Carl and Irene.

"I still say this is a bad idea," Tabby grumbled, as she stepped into the living room, where Donna waited on the couch.

"Should we do something special with your hair?" Donna asked. "We could pull it away from your face with some pretty pearl combs."

Tabby wrinkled her nose. "I like it plain. Besides, I'm not trying to make an impression on anyone." She flopped down next to Donna. "Even if I were, it would never work. Dad and Mom won't even know I'm alive once Lois shows up with her fiancé."

"I've got a great idea," Donna exclaimed. "Why don't you bring Roscoe to the barbecue? After we eat, you can entertain us with a cute little routine."

Tabby frowned. "You're kidding, right?"

"No. I think it would be a lot of fun. Besides, what better way to show your family that you really do have some talent?"

"Talent? What talent?"

"There you go again." Donna shook a finger in Tabby's face. "Self-doubting will never get you over being shy."

Tabby stood up. She knew Donna was probably right, but it was time to change the subject. "Do you think this outfit looks okay?" She brushed a hand across her beige-colored slacks.

"Well, now that you asked. . .I was thinking you might look better in that soft peach sundress of mine."

"No thanks. I'm going like I am, and that's final."

❧

The warm spring evening was a bit unusual for May in rainy Tacoma, but Tabby wasn't about to complain. The glorious weather was probably the only part of her birthday that would be pleasant.

The smoky aroma of hot dogs and juicy burgers sizzling on the grill greeted Tabby as she and Donna entered the Hartleys' backyard. Donna's father, wearing a long, white apron with a matching chef's hat, was busy flipping burgers, then covering them with tangy barbecue sauce. He stopped long enough to give both girls a quick peck on the cheek but quickly returned to the job at hand.

His petite wife, who looked like an older version of Donna, was setting the picnic table with floral paper plates and matching cups.

"Is th–there anything I can d–do to help?" Tabby questioned.

Irene waved her hand toward the porch swing. "Nope. I've got it all covered. Go relax, Birthday Girl."

"That's a good idea," Donna greed. "You swing, and I'll help Mom."

Tabby didn't have to be asked twice. The Hartleys' old porch swing had been her favorite ever since she was a child. Soon she was rocking back and forth, eyes closed, and thoughts drifting to the past.

She and Donna had spent many hours in the quaint but peaceful swing, playing with their dolls, making up silly songs, and whispering shared secrets. *If only life could have stayed this simple. If only I could always feel as contented as when I'm in this old swing.*

"Hey, Big Sister. . . Wake up and come to the party!"

Lois's shrill voice jolted Tabby out of her reverie, and she jerked her eyes open with a start. "Oh, I–I d–didn't kn–know you w–w–were here."

"Just got here." Lois gave Tabby an appraising look. "I thought you'd be a little more dressed for tonight's occasion."

Tabby glanced down at her drab slacks and pale yellow blouse, then she lifted her face to study Lois's long, pastel blue skirt, accented by a soft white silk blouse. By comparison, Tabby knew she looked like Little Orphan Annie.

Lois grabbed her hand and catapulted her off the swing. "Mom and Dad aren't here yet, but I want you to meet my fiancé, the successful lawyer, whose parents have big bucks."

Tabby was practically dragged across the lawn and over to the picnic table, where a dark-haired, distinguished-looking young man sat. A pair of stylish metal-framed glasses were perched on his aristocratic nose, and he was wearing a suit, of all things!

"Mike, Honey, this is the birthday girl—my big sister, Tabitha." Lois leaned over and dropped a kiss on the end of his nose.

He smiled up at her, then turned to face Tabby. "Hi. Happy birthday."

"Th–th–thanks," she murmured.

Michael gave her an odd look, but Lois grabbed his hand and pulled him off toward the porch swing before he could say anything more.

Donna, who had been pouring lemonade into the paper cups, moved toward Tabby. "Looks like your sister brought you over here just so she could grab the old swing."

Tabby watched her beautiful, self-assured sister swagger across the lawn, laughing and clinging to Michael like she didn't have a care in the world. She shrugged. "Lois can have the silly swing. She can have that rich boyfriend of hers too."

"Oh, oh. Do I detect a hint of jealousy?"

Tabby knew Donna was right, and she was about to say so, but her parents and grandmother had just come through the gate, and she figured it would be rude to ignore them.

"So glad you two could make it." Donna's father shook hands with Tabby's parents, then turned to her grandmother and planted a noisy kiss on her slightly wrinkled cheek. "You're sure lookin' chipper, Dottie."

"Carl Hartley, you still know how to pour on the charm, don't you?" Grandma Haskins raked a wrinkled hand through her short, silver-gray hair and grinned at him.

Up to this point, no one had even spoken to Tabby. She stood off to one side, head down, eyes focused on her beige sneakers.

Grandma Haskins was the first to notice her. "And here's our guest of honor. Happy twenty-fifth, Tabitha."

Tabby feigned a smile. "Th–thanks, Grandma."

"Yes, happy birthday," Mom added, placing a gift on one end of the table.

Tabby glanced up at her mother. She knew she looked a lot like Mom. They had the same mousy brown hair, dark brown eyes, and were both short of stature. That was where the similarities ended, though. Mom was much more socially secure than Tabby. She was soft-spoken, but unlike Tabby, her words didn't come out in a mumble-jumble of stammering and stuttering.

Tabby's gaze went to her father then. He was still visiting with Donna's dad and never even looked her way. Lois got her good looks from him, that was for sure. His blond hair, though beginning to recede, and those vivid blue eyes were enough to turn any woman's head. *No wonder Mom fell for Dad.*

Donna's mother, Irene, the ever-gracious hostess, instructed the guests to be seated at the picnic table, while she scurried about to serve them all beverages.

Even though Tabby was the only one in her family who professed Christianity, they all sat quietly through Carl's prayer. When he asked God to bless Tabby and give her many good years to serve Him, she heard Lois snicker.

Tabby had a compelling urge to dash back home to her apartment—where she'd be free of Lois's scrutiny and her dad's indifference. She knew it would be rude, and besides, the aroma of barbecued meat and the sight of several eye-catching salads made her feel as if she were starving. The promise of cake, ice cream, and gifts made her appreciate the special party Donna had planned too. It was more than her own family would have done. With the exception of Grandma, she doubted whether any of them even cared that today was her birthday.

"Please don't sing 'Happy Birthday' and make me blow out the dumb candles," Tabby whispered when Donna set a huge cake in front of her a short time later. It was a beautiful cake—a work of art, really—German chocolate, Tabby's favorite, and it was covered with thick cream-cheese frosting. Delicate pink roses bordered the edges, and right in the middle sat a giant-sized heart with the words, "Happy Birthday, Tabby."

"Don't spoil everyone's fun," Donna said softly.

Tabby bit back a caustic comeback, forcing herself to sit patiently through the strains of "Happy Birthday."

"Okay, it's time to open the presents." Donna moved the cake aside, then placed the gifts directly in front of Tabby. The first one was from Lois. Inside a gold foil-wrapped gift box was a pale green silk blouse and a makeup kit. It was filled with lipstick, blush, eyeliner, mascara, and a bottle of expensive perfume.

At Tabby's questioning look, Lois said, "I thought it might spark you up a bit. You always wear such drab colors and no makeup at all."

Tabby could have argued, since she did wear a touch of lipstick now and then. "Th—thanks, L—Lois," she mumbled instead.

Grandma Haskins reached over with her small gift bag. "Open mine next, Dear."

Tabby read the card first, then drew a small journal from the sack.

"I thought you might enjoy writing down some of your personal thoughts," Grandma explained. "I've kept a diary for many years, and I find it to be quite therapeutic."

Tabby and her maternal grandmother exchanged a look of understanding. Despite the fact that Grandma, who'd been widowed for the last ten years, wasn't a Christian, she was a good woman. Tabby felt that Grandma loved her, in spite of all her insecurities.

"Thank you, Grandma. I th—think it'll be f—fun."

"This one's from your folks," Donna said, pushing the other two gifts aside.

There was no card, just a small tag tied to the handle of the bag. It read: "To Tabitha, From Mom and Dad."

Tabby swallowed past the lump lodged in her throat. *They couldn't even write "love." That's because they don't feel any love for me. They only wanted me until Lois came along; then I became nothing but a nuisance.*

"Well, don't just sit there like a dunce. Open it!" her father bellowed.

Tabby ground her teeth together and jerked open the bag. Why did Dad always have to make her feel like such an idiot? As she withdrew a set of white bath towels, edged with black ribbon trim, her heart sank. Towels were always practical, but white? What in the world had Mom been thinking? She was sure it had been her mother's choice because Dad rarely shopped for anything.

"Th–thanks. Th–these will go g–good in our b–b–bathroom," she stuttered.

"I was hoping you'd put them in your hope chest," Mom remarked.

Tabby shook her head. "I d–don't have a h–hope chest."

"It's high time you started one then," Dad roared. "Lois is only nineteen, and she's planning to be married soon."

As if on cue, Lois smiled sweetly and held up her left hand.

"Your engagement ring is beautiful," Donna's mother exclaimed. "Congratulations to both of you."

Michael beamed and leaned over to kiss his bride-to-be.

Tabby blushed, as though she'd been kissed herself. Not that she knew what it felt like to be kissed. The only men's lips to have ever touched her face had been her dad's, when she was young, and Carl Hartley's, whenever he greeted her and Donna.

Donna cleared her throat. "Ah-hem! This is from Mom, Dad, and me." She handed Tabby a large white envelope.

Tabby's forehead wrinkled. Donna always went all out for her birthday. A card? Was that all she was giving her this year?

"Go ahead, open it," Donna coached. She was smiling like a cat who had just cornered a robin. Carl and Irene were looking at her expectantly too.

Tabby shrugged and tore open the envelope. She removed the lovely religious card that was signed, "With love, Donna,

Irene, and Carl." A small slip of paper fell out of the card and landed on the table, just missing the piece of cake Grandma Haskins had placed in front of Tabby. Tabby picked it up, and her mouth dropped open. "A gift certificate for a ventriloquist dummy?"

"Ventriloquist dummy?" Lois repeated. "What in the world would you need a dummy for?"

Before Tabby could respond, Donna blurted out, "Tabby's recently learned how to talk for two. She's quite good at it, I might add."

If ever there had been a time when Tabby wanted to find a hole to crawl into, it was now. She swallowed hard and said in a high-pitched squeak which sounded much like her puppet, "I–I'm just l–l–learning."

By the time Tabby and Donna returned to their apartment, Tabby's shock over the surprise gift certificate had worn off. It had been replaced with irritation. She knew Donna's heart was in the right place, and Tabby didn't want to make an issue out of it, but what in the world was she going to do?

Tabby placed her birthday gifts on the kitchen table and went out to the living room. Donna was busy closing the mini-blinds, and she smiled when she turned and saw Tabby. "I hope you enjoyed your party."

Tabby forced a smile in response. "It was nice, and I really do appreciate the expensive gift you and your folks gave me."

Donna nodded. "I sense there's a 'but' in there someplace."

Tabby flopped into the rocking chair and began to pump back and forth, hoping the momentum might help her conjure up the courage to say what was on her mind. "It was an expensive birthday present," she said again.

Donna took a seat on the couch, just opposite her. "You're worth every penny of it."

Tabby shrugged. "I don't know about that, but—"

"There's that 'but.' " Donna laughed. "Okay, let me have it. What don't you like about the idea of getting a professional ventriloquist dummy?"

Tabby stopped rocking and leaned forward. "I—uh—"

"Come on, Tabby, just spit it out. Are you mad because my folks and I gave you that certificate?"

"Not mad, exactly. I guess it really would be kind of fun to own a dummy, even if I'm only going to use it at the day care."

"That's exactly what I thought," Donna said with a satisfied smile.

"The gift certificate says it's redeemable at Beyers' Ventriloquist Studio."

"That's the only place in Tacoma where ventriloquist dummies are bought, sold, and repaired."

"I know, but Seth Beyers owns the business, and he—"

"Oh, I get it! You have a thing for this guy, and the thought of being alone with him makes you nervous."

Tabby bolted out of the rocking chair, nearly knocking it over. "I do not have a thing for him! I just can't go in there and talk to him alone, that's all. You know how hard it is for me to speak to anyone but you or the kids. Wasn't that obvious tonight at the party?" She began to pace the length of the living room. "I couldn't even get through a complete sentence without stuttering and making a complete fool of myself. No wonder my family thinks I'm an idiot."

Donna moved quickly to Tabby's side and offered her a hug. "You're a big girl now, Tabby. I can't go everywhere with you or always be there to hold your shaking hand."

Donna's words stung like fire, but Tabby knew they were spoken in love. "What do you suggest I do—call Seth Beyers and see if I can place an order over the phone?"

Donna shook her head. "Of course not. You need to take a look at what he's got in stock. If there isn't anything suitable, he has a catalog you can look through."

"But I'll stutter and stammer all over the place."

Donna stepped directly in front of Tabby. "I suppose you could always take little Roscoe along for added courage," she said with a teasing grin.

Tabby's face brightened. "Say, that's a great idea! I don't know why I didn't think of it myself!"

six

Tabby knew there was no point in procrastinating. If she didn't go to Beyers' Ventriloquist Studio right away, she'd have to endure the agony of Donna's persistent nagging. Since today was Friday, and she had an hour off for lunch, it might as well be now.

Tabby slipped Roscoe into the pocket of her raincoat, said good-bye to Donna, and rushed out the door. She stepped carefully to avoid several large puddles, then made a mad dash for her car, because, as usual, it was raining.

"Why couldn't it have done this last night?" she moaned. "Maybe then my birthday party would have been canceled." She slid into the driver's seat, closed the door with a bang, and pulled Roscoe out of her pocket. "Okay, little buddy, it's just you and me. I'm counting on you to get me through this, so please don't let me down."

❧

Seth had been up late the night before, putting the finishing touches on a grandpa dummy someone in Colorado had ordered from his catalog. He'd had trouble getting the moving glass eyes to shift to the right without sticking. Determined to see it through to completion, Seth had gone to bed shortly after midnight. Now he was feeling the effects of lost sleep and wondered if he shouldn't just close up shop for the rest of the day. He didn't have any scheduled customers that afternoon, and since it was raining so hard, it wasn't likely there would be any walk-ins, either.

Seth was heading over to put the "closed" sign in the window, when the door flew open, nearly knocking him off his

52

feet. Looking like a drenched puppy, Tabby Johnson stood there, holding her purse in one hand and a small, scruffy dog puppet in the other.

"Come in," he said, stepping quickly aside. "Here, let me take your coat."

"My—my c–coat is f–fine. It's w–w–waterproof."

Seth smiled, hoping to make her feel more at ease, but it didn't seem to have any effect on the trembling young woman. "I've been expecting you," he said softly.

"You—h–have?"

"Well, maybe not today, but I knew you'd be coming in sometime soon."

Tabby slipped Roscoe onto her hand and held him in front of her face. "How did you know Tabby would be coming here?" she made the puppet say.

Seth had no idea what she was up to, but he decided to play along. "Tabby's friend was in the other day," he answered, looking right at the puppet. "She bought a gift certificate for a dummy and said it was for Tabby's birthday."

Tabby's hand slipped slightly, and Roscoe's head dropped below her chin.

Now Seth could see her face clearly, and he had to force himself to keep talking to the puppet and not her. "Say, what's your name, little fellow?"

"Woof! Woof! I'm Roscoe Dog!"

She's actually doing ventriloquism, Seth noted. *Doing a pretty good job at it too. Should I compliment her? Maybe give her a few encouraging words about her newfound talent? No, I'd better play along for awhile and see if I can gain her confidence.*

Seth moved over to the counter where he usually did business with customers. He stepped behind it and retrieved one of his catalogs from the shelf underneath. "Are you planning to help Tabby pick out a dummy?" he asked, again directing his question to the puppet.

Roscoe's head bounced up and down. "Sure am. Have ya got anything on hand?"

"You don't want to look at the catalog?" This time Seth looked right at Tabby.

She squirmed under his scrutiny, but in a well-spoken ventriloquist voice she made the puppet say, "I'd rather see what you've got first."

Seth frowned. Tabby seemed unable to carry on a conversation without either stuttering or using the puppet, and she still hadn't looked him in the eye when he spoke directly to her. What was this little woman's problem, anyhow?

᠄

Tabby tapped the toe of her sneaker against the concrete floor as she waited for Seth's response to her request.

"Okay, I'll go in the back room and see what I can find," he finally mumbled. When Seth disappeared, she took a seat in one of the folding chairs near the front door. She didn't know what had possessed her to use Roscoe Puppet to speak to Seth Beyers. He probably thought she was out of her mind or acting like a little kid. If she'd tried to talk to him on her own, though, she'd have ended up stuttering like a woodpecker tapping on a tree. Tabby knew it was stupid, but using the puppet helped her relax, and she was able to speak clearly with no stammering at all. *Guess this little experience will be something to write about in my new journal,* she thought with a wry smile.

The telephone rang sharply, causing Tabby to jump. She glanced around anxiously, wondering whether Seth would hear it ringing and return to answer it. For a fleeting moment she thought of answering it herself but quickly dismissed the idea, knowing she'd only stutter and wouldn't have the foggiest idea of what to say.

She was rescued from her dilemma when Seth reappeared, carrying a large trunk, which he set on one end of the counter.

"Be right with you," he said, reaching for the phone.

Tabby waited impatiently as he finished his business. She was dying to know what was inside that huge chest.

Five minutes later, Seth finally hung up. "Sorry about the interruption. That was a special order, and I had to be sure of all the details."

Tabby moved back to the counter, waiting expectantly as Seth opened the trunk lid. "I didn't know if you wanted a girl, boy, or animal figure, so I brought a few of each," he explained. Tabby's eyes widened as Seth pulled out several dummies and puppets, placing them on the counter for her inspection.

"They all have open-close mouths and eyes that move from side to side. Would you like to try one?"

Roscoe was dropped to the counter as Tabby picked up a small girl dummy dressed in blue overalls and a pink shirt. The figure's moving glass eyes were blue, and her brown hair was braided. Tabby held the figure awkwardly with one hand, unsure of what to say or do with it. The telltale sign of embarrassment crept up the back of her neck, flooding her entire face with familiar heat. "H–how do you w–work it?"

"Here, let me show you." Seth moved quickly around the counter until he was standing right beside Tabby. She could feel his warm breath against her neck, and she shivered when his hand brushed lightly against her arm. She wondered if she might be coming down with a cold.

Seth pulled the slit on the dummy's overalls apart, so Tabby could see inside the hollow, hard plastic body. "See here. . .that's where the wooden control stick is hidden. You turn the rod to the right or left for the figure's head to move." He demonstrated, while Tabby held the dummy.

"When you want to make her talk, you need to pull sharply down on this." He gave the small metal handle a few tugs. "The right lever makes the eyes move from side to side."

When Tabby nodded, Seth stepped away, allowing her access to the inside of the figure's body. "Okay, now you try it."

The control stick felt stiff and foreign beneath Tabby's trembling fingers, and it took a few tries before she got the hang of it. "Hi, my name's Rosie," she made the dummy say in a high-pitched, little-girl voice. "Will you take me home with you?"

Tabby pretended to whisper something into the figure's ear.

"She wants to know how much I cost," Rosie said to Seth.

His sudden frown made Tabby wonder if the girl dummy cost a lot more than the value of her gift certificate.

"This little game has been fun," Seth said kindly, "but if we're gonna do business, I think Tabby should speak for herself."

Seth's words hadn't been spoken harshly, but they still had an impact, causing Tabby to flinch, as though she'd been slapped.

"I'm sorry, but I get in enough dummy talk of my own," he apologized. "I'd really like to speak to you one-on-one."

Tabby lifted her gaze to finally meet his, and their eyes met and held. "I–I h–have a ph–phobia about sp–speaking in p–public or to p–people I–I'm uncomfortable w–w–with."

Seth grinned, but his eyes remained serious. "I know all about phobias."

"Y–you do?"

"Yep. I studied them in one of my college psychology classes." He pointed at Tabby. "Your phobia is called phonophobia—fear of speaking aloud. I think everyone has at least one phobia, so it's really not such a big deal."

"W–we do? I m–mean, other p–people have ph–phobias, too?"

"Oh, sure. In fact, I believe I'm plagued with one of the worst phobias of all."

Tabby shot him a quizzical look. "R–really? W–what's your ph–ph–phobia?"

"It's arachibutyrophobia—peanut butter, sticking to the roof of my mouth."

She giggled, in spite of her self-consciousness. "Y–you're m–making that up."

He shook his head. "No, that's the correct terminology for my phobia."

Tabby eyed him suspiciously.

He raised his hand. "I'm completely serious. I really do freak out every time I try to eat peanut butter. If it gets stuck to the roof of my mouth, which it usually does, I panic."

If Seth was trying to put her at ease, it was working, because Tabby felt more relaxed than she had all day. She tipped her head toward Rosie. "So, h–how much does she cost?" she asked, stuttering over only one word this time.

"Three hundred dollars. Your gift certificate should pretty well cover it."

"W–what about tax?"

He rewarded her with a quick wink. "My treat."

"Oh, no, I c–couldn't let you do th–that."

Seth shrugged. "Okay. You treat me to a cup of coffee and a piece of pie, and we'll call it even."

"I–I have to get b–back to w–w–work," she hedged, beginning to feel less relaxed and fully aware that she was stuttering heavily again.

"You can give me your address and phone number, which I'll need for my customer records anyway," Seth said with a grin. "I'll come by your house tonight and pick you up."

Tabby's heartbeat picked up considerably. "P–p–pick me u–up?" Her knees felt like they could buckle at any moment, and she leaned heavily against the counter for support.

Seth's grin widened. "How's seven o'clock sound?"

She was keenly aware of his probing gaze, and it made her feel even more uneasy. All she could do was nod mutely.

"Great! It's a date!"

"How'd it go? Did you get a dummy? Where is it, and how come you don't look overjoyed?"

"You'd better go take your lunch break," Tabby said as she hung her wet raincoat over the back of a chair. "We can talk later."

Donna shook her head. "I ate with the kids, and now they're resting. We have plenty of time to talk."

With a sigh of resignation, Tabby dropped into one of the little chairs.

Donna pulled out the chair next to her and took a seat too. "Don't keep me in suspense a moment longer. Where's the dummy?"

"Right here," Tabby said, pointing to herself. "I'm the biggest dummy of all."

Donna's forehead wrinkled. "I don't get it."

"I'm supposed to take Seth Beyers out for pie and coffee tonight." Tabby's lower lip began to tremble, and her eyes filled with unwanted tears.

"You've got a date with Seth Beyers, and you're crying about it? I sure hope those are tears of joy."

Tabby dropped her head into her hands and began to sob.

"Please don't cry," Donna said softly. "I would think you'd be thrilled to have a date with someone as good-looking and talented as Seth."

Tabby sniffed deeply. "It's not really a date."

"It's not? What is it then?"

"He covered the tax for Rosie, so I owe him pie and coffee."

Donna shook her head. "I have absolutely no idea what you're talking about. Who's Rosie?"

Tabby sat up straight, dashing away the tears with the back of her hand. "Rosie's my new dummy. She's out in the car."

"Okay, I get that much. What I don't get is why you would owe Seth pie and coffee."

"I just told you. He covered the tax. My gift certificate was the right amount for the dummy, but not enough for the tax. Seth said if I treated him to pie and coffee, he'd call it even."

Donna smiled smugly. "Sounds like a date to me."

&

Seth had spent the better part of his day thinking about the pie and coffee date he'd made with Tabby. He wasn't sure why the thought of seeing the shy young woman again made his heart pound like a jackhammer. His mouth felt as though he'd just come from the dentist's office after a root canal. Maybe his interest in Tabby went deeper than a simple desire to help her climb out of the internal cell that obviously held her prisoner. If Seth were being completely honest, he'd have to admit that he was strangely attracted to Tabby. She might not be a beauty queen, but she was a long way from being ugly. In fact, he thought she was kind of cute. Even so, it wasn't her looks that held him captive. *What was it then?* he wondered.

Seth shrugged into a lightweight jacket and started out the door. "Guess I'll try to figure it all out tonight, over a piece of apple pie and a cup of coffee."

&

Tabby passed in front of her full-length bedroom mirror and stopped short. For a fleeting moment she thought she saw a smiling, beautiful woman staring back at her. No, that wasn't possible, because she was ugly. *Well, maybe not actually ugly,* she supposed. *Just ordinary. Shy and ordinary.* How could timid, stuttering Tabitha Johnson with mousy-colored brown hair and doe eyes ever look beautiful? Tabby's navy blue cotton dress slacks with matching blue flats weren't anything spectacular. Neither was the red-and-white pin-striped blouse she wore. She'd curled her hair for a change, and it fell in loose waves across her shoulders. It was nothing compared to her sister's soft, golden locks, though. What then, had caused her to think she looked beautiful?

Tabby studied her reflection more closely. A hint of pink

lipstick was all the makeup she wore. However, her cheeks glowed, and her eyes sparkled with. . .what? Excitement? Anticipation? What was she feeling as she prepared for this outing with Seth Beyers?

"Nervous, that's what I'm feeling!" Tabby exclaimed, pushing that elusive lock of hair away from her face. She reached for the doorknob. "Guess there's no turning back now. A promise is a promise," she muttered as she stepped into the living room. She began to pace, wondering if the butterflies, so insistent on attacking her insides, would ever settle down.

"Would you please stop pacing and sit down? You're making me nervous!" Donna patted the sofa cushion beside her. "Have a seat."

Tabby flopped onto the couch with a groan. "I hate waiting."

When the doorbell rang, Tabby jumped up like someone who'd been stung by a wasp. "Do you think I look okay?"

"You're fine. Now go answer that door."

As soon as Tabby opened the front door, her mouth went dry. Seth stood there, wearing a beige jacket, an off-white shirt, and a pair of brown slacks. His auburn hair looked freshly washed, and his green eyes sparkled with the kind of happiness she so often wished for. "Hope I'm not late," he said in a jovial tone.

"I–I th–think you're r–right on time."

"Are you ready to go?"

Tabby hesitated. "I—uh—let me g–get my d–dummy first."

Seth's eyebrows shot up. "I thought this was a pie and coffee thing." Without waiting for an invitation, he pushed past Tabby and sauntered into the living room. His gaze went to Donna, sitting on the couch. "You're Tabby's friend, right?"

She nodded. "Last time I checked."

"Can't you talk some sense into her?"

Donna shrugged and gave him a half-smile. "She's your date."

"Quit talking about me like I'm not even in the room!" Tabby shouted. "I need the dummy so I don't stutter."

Seth and Donna were both grinning at her. "What? What's so funny?" she hollered.

"You're not stuttering now," Seth said, taking a seat in the overstuffed chair nearest the door.

"I–I was angry," Tabby shot back. "I usually d–don't stutter when I'm mad."

Seth chuckled and gave Donna a quick wink. "Guess maybe we should keep her mad at us."

Donna wiggled her eyebrows. "You think that might be the answer?"

Tabby dropped to the couch. "Would you please stop? This is no l–laughing m–matter."

Donna looked at Seth and smiled, then she glanced back at Tabby. "Can't you see yourself sitting at the pastry shop, holding your dummy and talking for two?" She grabbed a throw pillow and held it against her chest, making a feeble attempt at holding back the waves of laughter that were shaking her entire body.

"You never know," Seth said with a chuckle. "We might draw quite a crowd, and Tabby could become famous overnight. I'd probably drum up some ventriloquist business in the process too."

Tabby didn't know whether to laugh or cry. She sat there several seconds, watching her best friend and so-called date, howling at her expense. When she'd had all she could take, Tabby jumped up and stormed out of the living room. Jerking open her bedroom door, she stalked across the carpet and flung herself on the bed. "I may never speak to Donna again," she wailed. "Forget about the dumb old tax. Seth Beyers can buy his own pie and coffee!"

seven

A stream of tears ran down Tabby's face, trickling toward her ears. She jumped off the bed, fully intending to go back into the living room and give Seth and Donna a piece of her mind, but she stopped short just after she opened the door.

"Tabby has real potential," she heard Donna say. "She's just afraid to use her talents."

"She needs lots of encouragement," Seth responded. "I can see how shy she is, but I didn't think taking the dummy along on our date would help her any. In fact, if someone were to laugh at Tabby, it might make things even worse. I really do want to help her be all she can be, but I'm not sure how to go about it."

"I think you're right," Donna said. "Taking the dummy along would be a bad idea."

Tabby peered around the corner. She could only see the back of Seth's head, but Donna was in plain view. She ducked inside her room. Now probably wasn't a good time to reappear. Not with the two of them talking about her.

Tabby crawled onto her bed again and stared at the ceiling. When she heard a knock at the door, she chose to ignore it. The door opened anyway, but she turned her face to the wall.

"Tabby, I'm sorry." The bed moved under Donna's weight, and Tabby felt a gentle hand touch her trembling shoulder. "Seth and I were wrong to laugh at you. It was all in fun, and we didn't expect you to get so upset."

Tabby released a sob and hiccupped. "Seth must think I'm a real dummy."

"I'm sure he doesn't. He only wants to help you."

Tabby rolled over, jerking into an upright position. "Help me? You mean he thinks I'm some kind of neurotic nut who needs counseling?" She swiped the back of her hand across her face. "Is he still here, or has he split by now?"

"He's still here."

Tabby bit her lip and closed her eyes with the strain of trying to get her emotions under control. "Just tell him the pie and coffee date is off."

Donna hopped off the bed and started for the door. "He's your date, not mine, so you can tell him yourself."

Tabby grabbed one of her pillows and let it sail across the room, just as the door clicked shut.

❧

Seth paced back and forth across the living room—waiting, hoping, praying Tabby would come out of her room. He needed to apologize for his rude behavior. The last thing he wanted was to hurt Tabby's feelings.

"Maybe I should have kept my big mouth shut and let her drag the dumb dummy along on our date. The worse thing that could have happened is we'd be the laughingstock of the pastry shop," he mumbled. "It sure wouldn't be the first time I've been laughed at. Probably not the last, either."

When Tabby's bedroom door opened, Seth snapped to attention. His expectancy turned to disappointment when Donna stepped from the room without Tabby. Seth began to knead the back of his neck. "She's really hoppin' mad, huh?"

Donna nodded. "Afraid so. She wouldn't even listen to me."

"Will she talk to me?"

Donna shrugged and took a seat on the couch. "I doubt it, Seth. She wanted me to tell you that the date is off, but I told her she'd have to tell you herself."

Seth chewed on his lower lip. "And?"

"She threw a pillow at me, but it hit the door instead."

Seth groaned. "She may be shy, but she's obviously got quite a temper."

Donna shook her head. "Not really. In fact, I've never seen her this angry before. She usually holds in her feelings. She must have it pretty bad."

Seth lowered himself into a chair. "Have what pretty bad?"

Donna opened her mouth to reply, but was stopped short when Tabby stepped into the room.

Seth could see she'd been crying. Her eyes were red, and her face looked kind of swollen. It made him feel like such a heel. He jumped up from his chair and moved swiftly toward her. "Tabby, I—"

She raised her hand, and he noticed she was holding a checkbook. He fell silent. It was obvious that a simple apology was not going to be enough.

&a.

Tabby shifted from one leg to the other, wondering what to say. She was keenly aware of Seth's probing gaze, and it made her feel uneasy. She was sure he already thought she was an idiot, so it shouldn't really matter what she said at this point. After tonight, Seth would probably never want to see her again anyway.

Tabby continued to stand there, shoulders hunched, arms crossed over her chest. She felt totally defeated. "Y–you h–hurt me," she squeaked. "You h–hurt me b–bad."

Seth nodded. "I know, and I'm sorry for laughing at you. It's just that—"

"You d–don't have to—to explain," Tabby said with a wave of her hand. "I know it w–would embarrass you if I t–took my d–dummy, but I can't t–talk right w–without her."

Seth took a few steps toward Tabby, which brought his face mere inches from hers. "Your stuttering doesn't bother me, but if you'd be more comfortable bringing Rosie, then I'm okay with it."

Tabby gulped and drew in a deep breath. She was sure Seth was only trying to humor her. Taking the dummy into the pastry shop would be even dumber than taking her puppet to Seth's place of business earlier that day. She held out her checkbook. "Let's forget about pie and coffee, okay? I'll write you a check to cover the tax due on Rosie."

Running a hand through his hair, Seth frowned. "You don't want to go out with me?"

She glanced at him anxiously, then dipped her head, afraid of the rejection she might see on his face. "I d–don't w–want to embarrass y–you."

"Look, if it would make you feel more at ease, we can get our pie and coffee to go. We could take it to the park and eat it in the car."

Tabby shifted uneasily. She really did want to go, but—

Donna, who'd been sitting silently on the couch, spoke up. "Would you just go already? You two are driving me nuts!"

"I th–think she w–wants to get rid of me," Tabby said, giving Seth a sidelong glance.

He wiggled his eyebrows playfully. "Her loss is my gain."

Tabby's heartbeat quickened at his sincere tone. He did seem to be genuinely sorry. "Okay, l–let's go. Without R–Rosie, though. One d–dummy is enough for y–you to h–handle."

"I hope you're not referring to yourself," he said with a puckered brow.

"She is," Donna said, before Tabby had a chance to answer. "She's always putting herself down."

Tabby shot her friend a look of irritation before retrieving her raincoat from the hall closet. "We'll talk about this later."

Donna shrugged. "You two have fun!"

"We will," Seth called over his shoulder.

❧

"I was impressed with your ventriloquism abilities when you were in my shop today," Seth said. He and Tabby were sitting in his black Jeep, at a viewpoint along the five-mile drive in Point Defiance Park.

Tabby took a sip of her mocha latte. "I'm just a beginner, and I know I still have lots to learn."

"But you're a quick learner. I saw no lip movement at all."

She shrugged. "That's what Donna's been telling me. She thinks I should do a ventriloquist routine for our Sunday school opening sometime."

Seth's face broke into a smile. "That's a terrific idea!"

"Oh, I couldn't."

"Why not?"

"I stutter."

Seth chuckled. "Not when you're really mad. . .or doing ventriloquism." He snapped his fingers. "Do you realize that you haven't stuttered once since we pulled into this parking spot? I don't know if it's the awesome sight of the lights on Narrows Bridge that has put you at ease, or if you're just beginning to feel more comfortable around me."

Tabby contemplated that for a few seconds. Seth was right; she hadn't been stuttering. For the first time all evening Tabby didn't feel nervous. In fact, she felt more relaxed than she had all day. Donna and the day care kids were the only people she'd ever felt this comfortable around. Maybe Seth could be her friend. Maybe. . .

Tabby grimaced. Who was she kidding? Seth was confident, good-looking, and talented. He'd never want someone like her as a friend. In his line of work, he met all sorts of people. Probably had lots of close friends. She was sure none of them stuttered or turned cherry red every time someone looked at them. Why did she allow herself to hope or have foolish dreams? Would she spend the rest of her life wishing for the impossible?

"Tabby, did you hear what I said?" Seth's deep voice broke into her thoughts, and she forced herself to look at him.

"Huh?"

He rested his palm on her trembling hand. "You don't have to be nervous around me. I'm just plain old Seth Beyers, fearful of eating sticky peanut butter."

Tabby swallowed hard. Seth's gentle touch made her insides quiver, and she looked away quickly, hoping to hide the blush she knew had come to her cheeks. At this moment, she felt as though *her* mouth was full of gooey peanut butter. How could she not be nervous when he was touching her hand and looking at her with those gorgeous green eyes? She closed her own eyes and found herself wondering how Seth's lips would feel against her own.

"My fear may not affect my relationship with people," Seth continued, "but it's real, nonetheless." He trailed his thumb across her knuckles, marching a brigade of butterflies through her stomach. "I'd like to be your friend, Tabby. I want to help you overcome your shyness. You have potential, and if you'll let Him, I know the Lord can use you in a mighty way."

Tabby blinked away stinging tears. How she wished it were true. She'd give anything to face the world with confidence. It would make her life complete if she could serve God without fear or bashfulness—even if it wasn't in a mighty way, like Seth was doing with his ventriloquist skills.

"Will you allow me to help?" Seth asked.

Tabby felt drawn to his compassionate eyes, and she sensed he could see right through her. *I could drown in that sea of green.*

"Tabby?"

She nodded. "I–I'm not expecting any big m–miracles, but yes, I w–would like your help."

❧

For the next several days Seth's offer of help played itself over and over in Tabby's mind. When he dropped her off at the apartment that night, after pie and coffee, he'd said he would give her a call, but he never explained how he planned to help her. Would he offer to get her speech therapy? If so, that would never work. Her parents had sent her for all kinds of therapy when she was growing up. Nothing helped. There wasn't a thing wrong with Tabby's speech. If there had been, she would have stuttered all the time, not just in the presence of those who made her feel uncomfortable. It was her low self-esteem and shyness that caused her to stutter, and she was sure there wasn't anything that could be done about it.

"You're awfully quiet today," Donna remarked, pulling Tabby out of her musings.

Tabby glanced over at her friend in the passenger seat. They took turns driving to work, and today they'd taken Tabby's car.

Tabby gave the steering wheel a few taps. "I was just thinking."

Donna laughed. "Thinking's okay, as long as you pay attention to where you're going."

"I am."

"Oh, yeah? Then how come you drove right past the church?"

Tabby groaned as she glanced to the left and saw the corner of Elm Street. She cranked the wheel and made a U-turn.

"Oh, great, now you're trying to get yourself a big, fat ticket," Donna complained. "What's with you this morning?"

"Nothing. I'm just preoccupied." Tabby pulled into the church parking lot and turned off the ignition.

"Thinking about Seth Beyers, I'll bet."

Tabby opened her mouth, but before she could get any words out, Donna cut her off. "I think that guy really likes you."

"Seth's just friendly. He likes everyone." Tabby didn't like where this conversation was going, and she'd have to steer it in another direction soon, or they might end up in an argument.

"I know Seth is friendly," Donna persisted, "but I think he's taken a special interest in you. You should have seen how upset he was when you ran into your room the other night."

"How about this weather? Can you believe it hasn't rained in the last half hour? We'd better get inside before it changes its mind and sends us another downpour."

Donna clicked her tongue. "You're trying to avoid the subject, and it won't work. I have something to say, and you're gonna hear me out."

"We'll be late for work."

Donna glanced at her watch. "We're ten minutes early. So, if you'll quit interrupting, we still have plenty of time to talk."

Tabby drew in a deep breath and let it out in a rush. "Okay, get whatever it is off your chest. I really want to get on with my day."

Donna gave her a reproachful look. "What I have to say isn't all that bad."

"All right then, let me have it."

Donna blinked. "My, my, you're sure testy. It's Seth, isn't it?"

Tabby remained silent.

"I really do think the guy likes you."

Tabby wrinkled her nose. "You already said that. I think Seth's the type of person who's kind to everyone. It's obvious that he takes his relationship with Christ seriously."

Donna raised her dark eyebrows. "And you don't?"

Tabby shrugged. "I try to, but I'm not outgoing and self-confident the way he is. I don't think I'm a very good Christian witness."

"You could be, Tabby. You have a wonderful new talent, which you should be using to serve the Lord."

"I–I still don't feel ready to do ventriloquism in front of a crowd."

"Maybe you need to take a few more lessons. I'm sure if you asked, Seth would be more than willing to help you."

Tabby drew in another long breath, and this one came out as a shuddering rasp. "He said he'd help, and I even agreed."

"That's great. I'm glad to hear it."

"I've thought it over thoroughly," Tabby said. "I like Seth too much to expect him to waste his time on someone like me."

Donna shook her head. "Now that's the most ridiculous thing I've ever heard. If you like the guy, then why not jump at any opportunity you have to be with him?"

"Aren't you getting this picture? I don't stand a chance with someone like Seth Beyers. He's totally out of my league."

Donna held up both hands. "I give up! You don't want to see your potential or do anything constructive to better yourself, so there's nothing more I can say." She jerked open the car door and sprinted off toward the church.

Tabby moaned and leaned against the headrest, "Maybe she's right. Maybe I need to pray about this."

eight

Seth had been thinking of Tabby for the past few days. In fact, he couldn't get her out of his mind. The other night she'd told him where she worked, and he had decided to stop by the day care for a little visit. One of the fringe benefits of being self-employed was the fact he could pretty much set his own hours and come and go whenever he felt like it. Today, he'd decided to take an early lunch and had put a note in his shop window saying he wouldn't be back until one.

Seth pulled his Jeep into the church parking lot, turned off the engine, and got out. He scanned the fenced-in area on one side of the building. There were several children playing on the swings, so he figured that must be part of the Caring Christian Day Care.

He ambled up the sidewalk, and was about to open the gate on the chain-link fence, when he caught sight of Tabby. She was kneeling on the grass, and a group of children sat in a semicircle around her, listening to a Bible story. The soft drone of her voice mesmerized him, as well as the kids, who were watching Tabby with rapt attention. She wasn't stuttering at all, he noticed. It was uncanny, the way she could speak so fluently with these children, yet stutter and hang her head in embarrassment whenever she was with him.

"And so, little ones," Tabby said as she closed the Bible. "Jonah truly learned his lesson that day."

"He never went on a boat again, right, Teacher?" a little red-haired, freckle-faced boy hollered out.

Tabby smiled sweetly, and Seth chuckled behind his hand. She still didn't know he was watching her, and he decided to keep it that way for a few more minutes.

"Jonah's lesson," Tabby explained, "was to obey God in all things. He could have drowned in that stormy sea, but God saved him by bringing the big fish along in time."

"I wonder if the fishy had bad breath," a little, blond-haired girl piped up.

Tabby nodded. "The inside of that fish probably smelled pretty bad, but Jonah was kept safe and warm for three whole days. When the fish finally spit him out on dry land, Jonah was happy to be alive."

"And I'll bet he never went fishing after that," said the freckle-faced boy.

Tabby laughed softly. Her voice sounded like music to Seth's ears. How could anyone so introverted around adults be so at ease with children? *She'll make a good mother some day,* Seth found himself thinking. *She has a sweet, loving spirit, and the kids seem to relate really well to her.*

Seth opened the gate and stepped inside the enclosure just as Tabby stood up. She brushed a few blades of grass from her denim skirt, and the children all stood too.

"It's time to go inside," she instructed. "Miss Donna is probably ready for us to bake those cookies now."

A chorus of cheering voices went up, and the kids, including those who had been swinging, raced off toward the basement door.

Tabby started to follow, but Seth cleared his throat loudly, and she whirled around to face him. "Oh, you—you sc–scared me. I d–didn't know you w–were h–here. How l–long have you–you been st–standing there?"

Seth grinned at her. "Just long enough to hear the end of a great story. The biblical account of Jonah and the big fish is one of my favorites."

"It's m–my favorite too," she murmured.

"You're really good with the kids," he said, nodding in the

direction of the disappearing pack of children.

"Th–thanks. I love w–working w–with them."

"It shows."

There was a moment of silence, as Seth stood there staring at Tabby, and she shifted from one foot to the other.

"Wh–what br–brings you here?" she finally asked.

"I came to see you," he said with a wide smile.

Her only response was a soft, "Oh."

"But now that I'm here, I think maybe I should follow the kids into the day care and see what kind of cookies they'll be making." Seth offered her a wink, and she blushed, dropping her gaze to her white sneakers.

"We're m–making chocolate ch–chip," Tabby said. "We'll be t–taking them to R–Rose Park Convalescent C–Center tomorrow m–morning."

He nodded. "Ah, so you're not only a great storyteller, but you're full of good deeds."

Her blush deepened, and she dipped her head even further. "It's n–nothing, really."

"I think you're too modest," Seth replied, taking a few steps toward her. When he was only inches away, he reached out and gently touched her chin. Slowly, he raised it, until her dark eyes were staring right into his. "There, that's better. It's kind of hard to carry on a conversation with someone who's staring at her feet."

Tabby giggled, obviously self-conscious, and it reminded him of one of her day care kids. "Wh–what did you w–want to see m–me about, Se–Se–Seth?"

"I thought maybe we could have lunch and talk about something," he answered, stepping away. "I saw a little deli just down the street, and I'm on my lunch hour, so—"

"Th–that would be nice, but I've got c–cookies to b–bake," she interrupted. "D–Donna and I w–will pr–probably be baking l–long after the k–kids go down for their n–naps."

Seth blew out his breath. "Okay, I guess I can call you later on. Will that be all right?"

She nodded. "Sure, th–that will be f–fine. Do y–you have m–my ph–phone number?"

"It's on the invoice I made out for your dummy purchase the other day."

"Oh." She turned toward the church. "I–I'd better g–get inside now. T–talk to you l–later, Seth."

He waved to her retreating form. "Yeah, later."

&

"You're wanted on the phone, Tabby!"

Tabby dried her hands on a towel and left the kitchen. When she entered the living room, Donna was holding the receiver, a Cheshire-cat grin on her pixie face.

"Who is it?"

"Seth."

Taking in a deep breath, Tabby accepted the phone, then motioned Donna out of the room.

Donna winked and sauntered into the kitchen.

"H–hello, Seth," Tabby said hesitantly. Her palms were so moist, she hoped she could hold onto the receiver.

"Hi, Tabby. How are you?"

"I'm o–okay."

"I'm sorry we couldn't have lunch today, but I said I'd call later. Is this a good time for you to talk?"

She nodded, then realizing he couldn't see her, she squeaked, "Sure, it's—it's f–fine."

"Good. You see, the reason I wanted to talk to you is, Saturday afternoon I'll be doing an advanced ventriloquism class," Seth said. "I was hoping you'd agree to come."

Tabby twirled the end of the phone cord between her fingers. "I—uh—really c–can't, Seth."

"Can't or won't?"

She flinched, wondering if Seth could read her mind.

"Tabby?"

"I–I wouldn't feel comfortable trying to do v–v–ventrilo-quism in front of a b–bunch of strangers," she answered truthfully. "You know h–how bad I stutter. They'd probably l–laugh at me."

There was a long pause, then, "How 'bout I give you some private lessons?"

"P–private lessons?"

"Sure. We could meet once a week, either at your apart-ment or in my shop."

"Well. . ."

"I'd really like to see your talent perfected. Besides, it would be a good excuse to be with you again."

He wants to be with me. Tabby squirmed restlessly. Did Seth really see her in some other light than a mere charity case? Could he possibly see her as a woman? An image of little Ryan O'Conner, the freckle-faced boy from day care, flashed through her mind. He had a crop of red hair, just like Seth. *I wonder if our son would look like that?*

"Tabby, are you still there?" Seth's deep voice drew Tabby back to their conversation.

"Yes, I'm—I'm h–here," she mumbled, wondering what on earth had been going on in her head. She hardly knew Seth Beyers, and fantasizing about a child who looked like him was absolutely absurd!

"Are you thinking about my proposal?" Seth asked, break-ing into her thoughts a second time.

"Pro–proposal?" she rasped. Even though she knew Seth wasn't talking about a marriage proposal, her heat skipped a beat. They'd only met a short time ago. Besides, they were exact opposites. Seth would never want someone as dull as her.

"So, what's it gonna be?" he prompted.

She sent up a silent prayer. *What should I do, Lord?* A few seconds later, as if she had no power over her tongue,

Tabby murmured, "O–okay."

"Your place or mine?"

Tabby caught a glimpse of Donna lurking in the hallway. "You could come here, but we'll probably have an audience."

"An audience?"

"Donna—my r–roommate."

Seth laughed. "Oh, yeah. Well, I don't mind, if it doesn't bother you."

Actually, the thought of Donna hanging around while Seth gave her lessons did make Tabby feel uncomfortable. It was probably preferable to being alone with Seth at his shop, though. "When do you w–want to b–begin?" she asked.

"Is tomorrow night too soon?"

She scanned the small calendar next to the phone. Tomorrow was Friday, and like most other Friday nights, she had no plans. "Tomorrow n–night will be f–fine. I d–don't get home 'til six-thirty or seven, and I'll need t–time to change and eat d–dinner."

"Let's make it seven-thirty then. See you soon, Tabby."

❧

Seth hung up the phone and shook his head. He could just imagine how Tabby must have looked during their phone conversation. Eyes downcast, shoulders drooping, hair hanging in her face.

His heart went out to her whenever she stuttered. He felt a hunger, a need really, to help the self-conscious little woman. He wanted to help her be all she could be. Maybe the advanced ventriloquism lessons would enable her to gain more confidence.

Seth turned away from the phone. *If I work hard enough, Tabby might actually become the woman of my dreams.* He slapped his palm against the side of his head. "Now where did that thought come from? I can't possibly be falling for this shy, introverted woman."

Back when he was a teen, Seth had made a commitment to serve God with his ventriloquist talents. He'd also asked the Lord for a helpmate—someone with whom he could share his life and his talent. Since he'd never found that perfect someone, maybe he could make it happen.

He sighed deeply. The way Tabby was now, he knew she'd only be a hindrance to his plans. He could just imagine what it would be like being married to someone who couldn't even talk to a stranger without stuttering or hiding behind a dummy. Unless he could draw her out of that cocoon, there was no possibility of them ever having a future together.

"What am I saying?" Seth lamented. "I hardly even know the woman, and I'm thinking about a future with her!" He shook his head. "Get a grip, Seth Beyers. She's just a friend—someone to help, that's all. You'd better watch yourself, because you're beginning to act like one of your dummies."

❧

"I don't know what you're so nervous about. You've already mastered the basic techniques of ventriloquism, so the rest should be a piece of cake," Donna said with a reassuring smile.

Tabby nodded mutely as she flopped onto the couch beside Donna. The truth was, she was a lot more nervous about seeing Seth than she was about perfecting her ventriloquism skills. She liked him—a lot. That's what frightened her the most. She'd never felt this way about a guy before. She knew her childish fantasies about her and Seth, and children who looked like him, were totally absurd, but she just couldn't seem to help herself.

"Tabby, the door!"

Donna's voice broke through Tabby's thoughts, and she jumped. She hadn't even heard the doorbell. "Oh, he's here? Let him in, okay?"

Donna grinned. "Since he's come to tutor you, don't you think *you* should answer the door?"

Tabby felt a sense of rising panic. "You're not staying, I hope."

"If you're gonna do ventriloquism, then you'll need an audience," Donna said.

The doorbell rang again, and Tabby stood up. When she opened the front door, she found Seth standing on the porch, little Rudy cradled in the crook of one arm, and a three-ring binder in his hand. "Ready for a lesson?"

She nodded, then motioned toward the living room. "We h–have our audience, j–just as I expected."

"That's okay. It's good for you to have an audience," Seth answered. "It'll give you a feel for when you're on stage."

Tabby's mouth dropped open. "On st–st–stage?"

Seth laughed. "Don't look so worried. I'm not suggesting you perform for a large crowd in the next day or two. Some-day you might, though, and—"

"No, I won't!" Tabby shouted. "I'm only d–doing this so I can per–perform better for the kids at the d–day care."

Seth shrugged. "Whatever." He followed her into the living room. "Where's your dummy?"

"In my room. I'll go get her." Tabby made a hasty exit, leaving Seth and Donna alone.

❧

"She's a nervous wreck," Donna remarked as Seth placed the notebook on the coffee table, then took a seat on the couch.

"Because you're here?"

She shook her head. "I think you make her nervous."

"Me? Why would I make Tabby nervous?"

"Well, I'm pretty sure. . ."

"I–I'm ready," Tabby announced as she entered the room carrying Rosie.

Seth stood up. "Great! Let's get started."

"Sh–should I sit or st–stand?"

"However you're the most comfortable." Seth nodded

toward the couch. "Why not sit awhile, until you're ready to put on a little performance for us?"

"I–I may never be r–ready for that."

"Sure you will," Seth said with assurance. He wanted her to have enough confidence to be able to stand up in front of an audience, but from the way she was acting tonight, he wondered if that would ever happen.

"Tabby, show Seth how you can make Rosie's head turn backwards," Donna suggested.

Tabby dropped to the couch and held her dummy on one knee. She inserted her hand in the opening at the back of the hard plastic body and grabbed the control stick. With a quick turn of the stick, Rosie was looking backwards. "Hey, where'd everybody go!" the childlike voice squealed.

Not one stuttering word, Seth noted, as he propped one foot on the footstool by Donna's chair. *Talking for two seems to be the best way Tabby can converse without stammering.* "We're right here, Rosie. Come join the party." This came from Rudy Right, who was balanced on Seth's knee.

"Party?" Rosie shot back. "We're havin' a party?"

"Sure, and only dummies are invited." Rudy gave Tabby a quick wink.

She giggled, then made Rosie say, "Guess that means we'll have to leave, 'cause the only dummies I see are pullin' someone else's strings."

Seth chuckled. "I think we've been had, Tabby." He scooted closer to her. "Would you like to learn a little something about the near and far voice?"

"Near and far? What's that?" The question came from Donna.

"The near voice is what you use when your dummy is talking directly to you or someone else. Like Tabby and I just did with our two figures," Seth explained. "The far voice would be when you want your audience to believe they're hearing the dummy talking from someplace other than directly in front of them." He pointed to the telephone on the table by the couch. "Let's say you just received a phone call from your dummy, and you want the audience to hear the conversation." Seth reached over and grabbed the receiver off the hook.

"Hi, Seth, can I come over?" A far-sounding, high-pitched voice seemed to be coming from the phone.

"Sure, why don't you?" Seth said into the receiver. "We're having a party over at Tabby and Donna's tonight, so you're more than welcome to join us."

"That's great! I love parties!" the far voice said. "Be right there!"

Seth hung up the phone and turned to face Tabby. "Do you have any idea how I did that?"

"You used the power of suggestion," Donna said, before Tabby had a chance to open her mouth. "We saw a phone and heard a voice, so it makes sense that we thought the sound was coming from the receiver."

Seth looked at Tabby. "What do you think?"

"I–I'm not sure, but I think m–maybe you did something different in your th–throat."

Seth grinned. "You catch on fast. I tightened my vocal chords so my voice sounded a bit pinched or strained. There's an exercise you can do to help make this sound."

"Oh, great! I love to exercise," Donna said, slapping her hands together.

Seth could tell from Tabby's expression that she was more than a bit irritated with Donna's constant interrupting. He wished there was some way to politely ask her well-meaning friend to leave.

"Actually, Donna, it's not the kind of exercise you're thinking of. It's only for ventriloquists, so. . ."

Donna held up both hands. "Okay, I get the picture. You

want me to keep my big mouth shut, right?"

"You are kind of a nuisance," Tabby replied.

Wow, she can get assertive when she wants to. Seth wondered what other talents lay hidden behind Tabby's mask of shyness.

"I'll keep quiet," Donna promised.

Tabby raised her eyebrows at Seth, and he grinned in response. "Now, let's see. . . Where were we?"

"An exercise." Donna ducked her head. "Sorry."

"The first thing you do is lean over as far as you can," Seth said as he demonstrated. "Try to take in as much air as possible, while making the *uh* sound."

Tabby did what he asked, and he noticed her face was turning red. How much was from embarrassment and how much from the exercise, he couldn't be sure, but he hoped it wouldn't deter her from trying.

"Now sit up again and try the same amount of pressure in your stomach as you make the *uh* sound." He placed one hand against his own stomach. "You'll need to push hard with these muscles as you speak for your far-sounding voice. Oh, and one more thing. It's best to keep your tongue far back in your mouth, like when you gargle. Doing all that, try talking in a high, whisper-like voice."

"Wow, that's a lot to think about all at once!" The comment came from Donna again, and Seth wondered if Tabby might be about to bolt from the room.

"There is a lot to think about," he agreed, "but with practice, it gets easier." He leaned close to Tabby and whispered, "Ready to try it now?"

She sucked in her bottom lip and nodded. "Hi, I'm glad you're home. I was afraid nobody would answer the phone."

Seth grabbed her free hand and gave it a squeeze. "That was awesome, Tabby! You catch on quick. A natural born ventriloquist, that's what you are."

A stain of red crept to her cheeks, but she looked pleased. "Th–thanks."

Seth pulled his hand away and reached for the notebook he'd placed on the coffee table. "I have some handout sheets to give you. Things for you to practice during this next week and a few short distant-voice routines to work on."

Tabby only nodded, but Donna jumped up and bounded across the room. "Can I see? This has all been so interesting! I'm wondering if maybe I should put away my art supplies and come back to your shop to look at dummies." She grinned at Tabby. "What do you say? Should I take up ventriloquism so we can do some joint routines?"

nine

By the time Tabby closed the door behind Seth, she felt emotionally drained and physically exhausted. Tonight's fiasco would definitely be recorded in that journal Grandma had given her. Donna had done nothing but interrupt, offer dumb opinions, and flirt with Seth. At least that's how Tabby saw it. Her best friend was obviously interested in the good-looking ventriloquist. What other reason could she have for making such a nuisance of herself?

Well, she's not going to get away with it, Tabby fumed. She headed for the living room, resolved to make things right. *Friend or no friend, I'm telling Donna exactly what I think.*

Donna was sitting on the couch, fiddling with the collar on Rosie's shirt. "You know what, Tabby? I think your dummy might look cuter in a frilly dress. You could curl her hair and—"

"Rosie looks just fine the way she is!" Tabby jerked the ventriloquist figure out of Donna's hands and plunked it in the rocking chair. "I'd appreciate it if you'd mind your own business too."

Donna blinked. "What's your problem? I wasn't hurting Rosie. I was only trying to help."

Tabby moved toward the window, though she didn't know why. It was dark outside, and there was nothing to look at but the inky black sky. "I've had about enough of your opinions to last all year," she fumed.

Donna joined Tabby at the window. "I thought your lesson went really well. What's got you so uptight?"

83

Tabby turned to face her. "I'm not uptight. I'm irritated."

"With me?"

Tabby nodded. "You like him, don't you?"

"Who?"

"Seth. I'm talking about Seth Beyers!"

Donna tipped her head. "Huh?"

"Don't play dumb. You know perfectly well who I mean, and why I think you like him."

"I think Seth's a nice guy, but—"

"Are you interested in him romantically?"

"Romantically?" Donna frowned. "You've gotta be kidding."

Tabby sniffed deeply. "No, I'm not. You hung around him all night and kept asking all sorts of dumb questions."

Donna's forehead wrinkled. "You're really serious, aren't you?"

"I sure am."

"I think we'd better have a little talk about this. Let's sit down." Donna motioned toward the couch.

Tabby didn't budge. "There's nothing to talk about."

"I think there is."

"Whatever," Tabby mumbled with a shrug.

Donna sat on the couch, but Tabby opted for the rocking chair, lifting Rosie up, then placing the dummy in her lap after she was seated.

"I'm not trying to steal your guy," Donna insisted. "He's not my type, and even if he were, you should know that I'd never sabotage my best friend."

The rocking chair creaked as Tabby shifted, then she began to pump her legs back and forth. "Seth is not my guy."

A smile played at the corner of Donna's lips. "Maybe not now, but I think he'd like to be."

Tabby folded her arms across her chest and scowled. "Fat chance."

"There might be, if you'd meet him halfway."

"Like you did tonight—with twenty questions and goofy remarks?"

"I was only trying to help."

"How?"

"Before Seth arrived, you said you were nervous."

"And?"

"I was trying to put you at ease."

"By butting in every few minutes?" Tabby gulped and tried to regain her composure. "How was that supposed to put me at ease?"

Before Donna could say anything, Tabby stood up. "All you succeeded in doing tonight was making me more nervous."

"Sorry."

Donna's soft-spoken apology was Tabby's undoing. She raced to the couch, leaned over, and wrapped her friend in a bear hug. "I'm sorry too. I–I'm just not myself these days. I think maybe I. . ." Her voice trailed off, and she blinked away tears, threatening to spill over. "Let's forget about tonight, okay?"

Donna nodded. "Just don't let it ruin anything between you and Seth."

Tabby groaned. "There's nothing to ruin. As I said before, there isn't anything going on. Seth and I are just friends— at least I think we are. Maybe our relationship is strictly business."

Donna shrugged. "Whatever you say."

"I think I'll take my next ventriloquist lesson at Seth's shop," Tabby said as she started toward her room. "Tonight made me fully aware that I'm not even ready for an audience of one yet."

❧

Seth wasn't the least bit surprised when Tabby called the following week and asked to have her next lesson at his place of business. Her friend, Donna, had turned out to be more than a helpful audience, and he was sure that was the reason for the change of plans. The way he saw it, Donna had actually been a deterrent, and it had been obvious that her constant interruptions made Tabby uptight and less able to grasp what he was trying to teach her. Even though they might be interrupted by a phone call or two, Beyers' Ventriloquist Studio was probably the best place to have Tabby's private lessons.

A glance at the clock told Seth it was almost seven. That was when Tabby had agreed to come over. His shop was closed for the day, so they should have all the privacy they needed.

"She'll be here any minute," he mumbled. "I'd better get this place cleaned up a bit."

Not that it was all that dirty, but at least it would give him something to do while he waited. If things went really well, he planned to ask her on a date, and truthfully, he was more than a little anxious about it. What if she turned him down? Could his male ego take the rejection, especially when he'd planned everything out so carefully?

Seth grabbed a broom out of the storage closet and started sweeping up a pile of sawdust left over from a repair job he'd recently done on an all-wooden dummy brought in a few weeks ago.

As he worked, he glanced over at Rudy Right, sitting in a folding chair nearby. "Well, little buddy, your girlfriend, Rosie, ought to be here any minute. I sure hope you're not as nervous as I am."

The wooden-headed dummy sat motionless, glass eyes staring straight ahead.

"So you're not talking today, huh?" Seth said with a shake of his head. "I'll bet you won't be able to keep your slot jaw shut once Tabby and her vent pal arrive."

Talking to Rudy like this was nothing new for Seth. He found that he rather enjoyed the one-way conversation. It was good therapy to talk things out with yourself, even if you were looking at a dummy when you spoke. He was glad there was no one around to witness the scene, though. If there had been, he might be accused of being a bit eccentric.

Seth chuckled. "Maybe I am kind of an oddball, but at least I'm having fun at my profession."

The bell above his shop door jingled, disrupting his one-way conversation. He grinned when Tabby stepped into the room, carrying Rosie in her arms. "Hi, Tabby."

"I–I hope I'm not l–late," she said. "Traffic was r–really bad."

Seth glanced at the clock again. "Nope, you're right on time."

"Are—are you r–ready for my l–lesson? You l–look kind of b–busy."

"Oh, you mean this?" Seth lifted the broom. "I was just killing time 'til you got here. My shop gets pretty dirty after I've been working on a dummy."

She nodded. "I g–guess it w–would."

Seth put the broom back in the closet and turned to face Tabby. "Are you ready for lesson number two?"

"I–I th–think so."

"Let's get started then." He motioned toward one of the folding chairs. "Have a seat and I'll get my notes."

&

Tabby watched as Seth went to his desk and shuffled through a stack of papers. *Why is he taking time out of his busy schedule to work with me?* she asked herself. *I'm sure he has much better things to do than give some introverted, stuttering woman private ventriloquist lessons.*

"Okay, all set." Seth dropped into a chair and graced her with a pleasant smile. "Did you get a chance to practice your near and far voices?"

"I p–practiced a little."

"How about a demonstration then?"

"N–n–now?"

"Sure, now's as good a time as any." Seth pointed at Rosie.

"If it would be any easier, you can talk through her instead of a pretend object or the telephone."

"How c–can I do th–that?" Tabby asked. "If I t–talk for R–Rosie, won't that be m–my near v–voice?"

Seth scratched his head. "Good point. I'll tell you what—why don't you set Rosie on a chair across the room, then talk for her. Make it sound as though her voice is coming from over there, and not where you're sitting."

Tabby bit down on her bottom lip and squeezed her eyes tightly shut. She wasn't sure she could do what Seth was asking, and she certainly didn't want to make a fool of herself. She'd already done that a few times in Seth's presence.

"You can do this," Seth urged. "Just give it a try."

Tabby opened her eyes and blew out the breath she'd been holding. "All r–right." She stood up and carried Rosie and a chair across the room, then placed the dummy down and returned to her own seat. "Hey, how come you put me way over here?" she made Rosie say in a childlike voice.

"You're in time-out."

"That's not fair, I'm just a dummy. Dummies should never be in time-out."

"Oh, and why's that?"

"Dummies are too dumb to know how to behave."

Tabby opened her mouth, but Seth's round of applause stopped her. She turned to look at him and was surprised when he gave her "thumbs-up."

"D–did I do o–okay?"

He grinned from ear to ear. "It was more than 'okay.' It was fantastic, and you never stuttered once. I'm proud of you, Tabby."

Tabby could feel the warmth of a blush as it started at her neckline and crept upward. She wasn't used to such compliments and was unsure how to respond.

"In all the years I've been teaching ventriloquism, I don't

think I have ever met anyone who caught on as quickly as you," Seth said sincerely. "You mastered the basics like they were nothing, and now this—it's totally awesome!"

"You really th–think so?"

"I know so. Why, you—"

Seth's words were cut off when the shop door opened, jingling the bell. In walked Cheryl Stone, the attractive redhead who had demonstrated her talents at Seth's beginning ventriloquism workshop, where Tabby first met him.

Cheryl gave Seth a smile so bright Tabby was sure the sun must still be shining. "Hi, Seth, I was in the neighborhood and saw your lights on. I was wondering if you've finished that new granny figure for me yet?"

Seth gave Tabby an apologetic look. "Sorry about the interruption," he whispered. "I wasn't expecting anyone else tonight, and I forgot to put the closed sign in my window."

"It's o–okay," Tabby murmured. "I'll j–just w–wait over th–there with R–Rosie w–while you take c–care of b–business." She was stuttering heavily again, and it made her uncomfortable.

Seth nodded. "This will only take a minute."

Tabby moved quickly toward Rosie, hoping Cheryl wouldn't stay long. She watched painfully as the vibrant young woman chatted nonstop and batted her eyelashes at Seth. *She likes him, I can tell. I wonder if they've been seeing other socially.*

Tabby shook her head. It was none of her business who Seth chose to see. Besides, if she were being totally honest, she'd have to admit that Seth and Cheryl did make a striking pair. They were both redheads, had bubbling personalities, and could do ventriloquism. What more could Seth ask for in a woman?

ten

It was nearly half an hour later when Cheryl finally walked out the door. Seth gave Tabby an apologetic look. "Sorry about that. Guess she's a little anxious to get her new dummy." He offered Tabby one of the most beautiful smiles she'd ever seen. "Before we continue with your lesson, I'd like to ask you a question."

Her heart quickened. Why was he staring at her that way? She swallowed against the tightening in her throat. "What question?" she squeaked.

Seth dropped into the seat beside her. "I have to go to Seattle tomorrow—to pick up an old dummy at the Dummy Depot. I was wondering if you'd like to go along."

Tabby's mouth went dry. He was asking her to go to Seattle. Was this a date? No, it couldn't be. Seth wouldn't want to go out with someone as plain as her. Why didn't he ask someone like cute Cheryl Stone? From the way the redhead kept flirting with him, Tabby was sure she would have jumped at the chance.

"Tabby?" Seth's deep voice cut into her thoughts.

"H–huh?"

"Are you busy tomorrow? Would you like to go to Seattle?"

She blinked. "Really? You w–want m–me to go along?"

He nodded. "I thought after I finish my business at the Dummy Depot we could go down by the waterfront. Maybe eat lunch at Ivar's Fish Bar and check out some of the gift shops along the wharf. I think it would be fun, don't you?"

Tabby gazed at the floor as she mulled this idea over. Tomorrow was Saturday. She wouldn't be working, and she had no other plans. She hadn't been to the Seattle waterfront in ages. Despite the amount of people usually there, it wasn't closed in the way so many of the buildings in Seattle Center were. The waterfront was open and smelled salty like the sea. Besides, it was an opportunity to spend an entire day with Seth.

"Tabby?"

She looked up. "Y–yes. I'd l–like to go."

❧

Tabby didn't sleep well that night. Excitement over spending a whole day with Seth occupied her thoughts and kept her tossing and turning. She was sure Seth wouldn't appreciate her taking Rosie to talk through, but she was concerned about her stuttering. Seth had told her several times that her speech impediment didn't bother him. It bothered her, though—a lot. She'd have given nearly anything to be confident and capable like normal people.

If only God hadn't made me so different, she wrote in her journal before turning off the light by her bed.

Tabby let her head fall back as she leaned into the pillow. *Maybe it wasn't God who made me different. It's all Lois's fault. If she just wasn't so beautiful and confident—everything Mom and Dad want in a daughter—everything I'm not.* She squeezed her eyes tightly shut. *Guess I can't really blame Lois, either. She can't help being beautiful and confident. It would take a miracle to make Mom and Dad love me the way they do her. They think I'm a failure.*

The thrill of her upcoming date with Seth was overshadowed by pain. She needed to work on her attitude. It wasn't a good Christian example, not even to herself. She released a shuddering sigh, whispered a short prayer asking God to help her accept things as they were, then drifted off to sleep.

❧

When Tabby entered the kitchen the following morning, she found Donna sitting at the table, sketching a black-and-white picture of a bowl of fruit.

"All ready for your big date?"

Tabby shrugged. "It's not a real date."

"What would you call it?"

"I'd call it a day in Seattle to—" She giggled. "Maybe it is kind of a date."

Donna laughed too. "You came home last night all excited about going, and it sure sounded like a date to me. I'm kind of surprised, though."

"About what?"

"I didn't think you liked Seattle."

Tabby dropped into a chair. "I don't like the Seattle Center, or shopping downtown, but we're going to the waterfront. I love it there, even with all the people."

Donna grinned. "I think you'd go to the moon and back if Seth Beyers was going."

"Don't even go there," Tabby warned. "I've told you before, Seth and I are just friends."

Donna shrugged. "Whatever you say."

Tabby glanced at the clock above the refrigerator. "Seth will be here in an hour, and I still need to eat breakfast, shower, and find something to wear." She reached for a banana from the fruit bowl in the center of the table.

"Hey! You're destroying my picture! Why don't you fix a fried egg or something?"

Tabby pulled the peal off the banana and took a bite. "Eggs have too much artery-clogging cholesterol. Fruit's better for you." She glanced at Donna's drawing. "Besides, you've already got some bananas sketched, so you shouldn't miss this one."

Donna puckered her lips. "You never worry about cholesterol when you're chomping down a burger or some greasy fries."

Tabby gave her a silly grin. "Guess you've got me there."

"How'd the lesson go yesterday? You never really said," Donna asked.

Tabby was tempted to tell her about Cheryl's interruption and how much it had bothered her to see the two redheads talking and laughing together. She knew it would only lead to further accusations about her being interested in Seth.

She flicked an imaginary piece of lint from the sleeve of her robe and replied, "It went fine."

"Great. I'm glad."

Tabby felt a stab of guilt pierce her heart. She was lying to her best friend. Well, not lying exactly, just not telling the whole story. "Seth got an unexpected customer, and we were interrupted before we really got much done."

"But you continued on with the lesson after they left, didn't you?"

Tabby grabbed an orange from the fruit bowl and began to strip away the peel. "The customer was a redheaded woman named Cheryl. I think Seth likes her."

"But it's you he invited to Seattle," Donna reminded.

"He probably feels sorry for me."

Donna dropped her pencil to the table. "Is there any hope for you at all?"

Tabby sighed. "I wish I knew. Sometimes I think there might be, and other times I'm so full of self-doubts."

"What makes you think Seth likes this redhead, anyway?" Donna asked.

"She's cute, talented, and outgoing. What guy wouldn't like that?" Tabby wrinkled her nose. "They looked like a pair of matching bookends."

Donna snickered. "Well, there you have it! If Seth can look at this redheaded gal and see himself, then he's bound to fall head over heels in love with her."

Tabby pushed away from the table. "Seth and Cheryl make a perfect couple, and I'm just a millstone around Seth's neck."

"If he saw you as a millstone, he sure wouldn't be asking you out. Normal people don't go around asking millstones to accompany them to Seattle for the day."

Tabby stared off into space. "Maybe you're right."

❧

Seth arrived on time. Not wishing to give Donna the chance to say anything to him, Tabby raced out the front door and climbed into his Jeep before he even had a chance to get out.

"I was planning to come in and get you," Seth said as she slid into the passenger seat.

She smiled shyly. "That's okay. I was r–ready, so I f–figured I may as w–well s–save you the b–bother."

Seth smiled. "You look nice and comfortable."

Tabby glanced down at her faded blue jeans and peach-colored sweatshirt, wondering if she was dressed too casually. Maybe she should have chosen something else. She considered Seth for a moment. He was wearing a pair of perfectly pressed khaki-colored pants and a black polo shirt. His hair was combed neatly in place, parted on the left side. He looked way too good to be seen with someone as dowdy as her.

"So, w–where exactly is th–this Dummy Depot, and w–what kind of d–dummy are you b–buying there?" she asked, hoping to drag her thoughts away from how great Seth looked today.

Seth pulled away from the curb. "The Dummy Depot sells mostly used dummies. Harry Marks, the guy who runs the place, recently got one in that needs some repairs. He asked if I'd come get it, since his car isn't running and he didn't want to catch a bus to Tacoma. I thought it might be kind of nice to mix a little pleasure with business," Seth said, giving Tabby another one of his heart-melting smiles.

Tabby nodded. "Makes sense to me." She leaned her head against the headrest and released a contented sigh. Maybe he really did want to be with her. Maybe there was a chance that. . .

"Have you known Donna long?" Seth asked, breaking into her thoughts.

"Huh?"

"How long have you and Donna been friends?"

"Ever since we w–were kids. Her folks m–moved next-door to us when we were b–both two."

"Tell me a little about your family," he pried.

"There's nothing m–much to tell."

"There has to be something." Seth tapped the steering wheel with his long fingers. "Do your folks live nearby? Do you have any brothers and sisters?"

Tabby swallowed hard. The last thing she wanted to do was talk about her family. This was supposed to be a fun day, wasn't it? "My—uh—p–parents live in Olympia, and I h–have one s–sister. She l–lives in a high-rise apartment in d–downtown Tacoma, and sh–she's a secretary. There's n–nothing m–more to tell."

"You're lucky to have a sister," Seth commented. "I grew up as an only child. My folks were killed in a car wreck when I was fourteen, and my grandparents took me in."

"I'm so s–sorry," she murmured.

"Grandma and Grandpa Beyers were good to me, though. They taught me about Christ and helped me learn to use my talents for Him." Seth smiled. "I'll never forget the day Grandpa informed me that when he and Grandma were gone, the house would be mine."

Tabby knew the house he was referring to was the one he lived in now. The basement had been converted into his ventriloquist shop. Seth had told her that much when she'd had her lesson the evening before. What he hadn't told her was that the house had been his grandparents', or that they'd passed away.

"I'm s–sorry your g–grandparents aren't l–living anymore. It must be h–hard not to h–have any family," she said with feeling. As much as she disliked many of the things her own family said or did, she couldn't imagine what it must have been like growing up as an only child or not having her parents around at all, even if they did make her feel like dirt most of the time.

Seth chuckled. "Grandma and Grandpa aren't dead yet."

"They're n–not?"

"No, they moved into a retirement home a few years ago. Said the old house was too much for them to handle." Seth cast her a sidelong glance. "Grandpa thought the place would be well suited to my business, not to mention a great place to raise a bunch of kids someday."

Tabby wasn't sure how to respond to that statement. She'd always dreamed of having a big family herself, but the possibility didn't seem very likely.

"There sure is a l–lot of traffic on the f–freeway today, isn't there?" she said, changing the subject again.

Seth nodded. "Always is a steady flow of cars on I–5, but the weekends are even worse. Things will level off a bit once we get away from the city."

Tabby turned to look out the passenger window. They had just entered the freeway and were traveling over a new overpass. As busy as the freeway was here, she knew it would be even worse once they got closer to Seattle. It made her thankful Seth was driving. She'd be a ball of nerves if she were in the driver's seat.

"Mind if I put a cassette in the tape player?" Seth asked.

"Go a–ahead."

When the soft strains of a familiar Christian song came on, Tabby smiled. Seth liked the same kind of music she did. She closed her eyes and felt her body begin to relax. She wasn't sure if it was because of Seth's rich baritone accompanying the tape, or simply the fact that she was with him today. Tabby was glad she'd accepted Seth's invitation to go to Seattle.

❧

Seth glanced over at Tabby. Her eyes were shut, and she was sitting silent and still. He wished he could read her mind. Find out what thoughts were circling around in her head. *She reminds me of a broken toy. She didn't have much to say about her family. I wonder if something from her past is the reason for her terrible shyness. If she's hurting, then maybe her heart can be mended. There's even a chance she could actually be better than new.*

The only trouble was, Seth wasn't sure how to find out what kind of pain from the past held Tabby in its grip. She was a mystery he wanted to solve. Since Tabby seemed so reserved and unable to communicate her feelings to him, maybe he should talk to Donna about it. Tabby said they'd been friends most of their lives. Surely Donna would know what made Tabitha Johnson tick. A little bit of insight might help him know what direction to take in making her over into his perfect woman.

Seth hugged the knowledge to himself and smiled. *As soon as I get the chance, I'll get together with Donna and find out what gives.*

eleven

The Dummy Depot was located in downtown Seattle, in a small shop near the busy shopping area. While Seth talked business with the owner, Tabby walked around the room studying all the figures for sale. It didn't take long to realize she could have bought a used dummy for half the price she'd paid for Rosie. She consoled herself with the fact that most of the figures looked well-used and had lost their sparkle. Rosie, on the other hand, was brand new, without a scratch, dent, or paint chip on her entire little body. Besides, she'd purchased the dummy with the birthday gift certificate from Donna and her parents. They'd wanted her to have a new one or else they wouldn't have given it to her.

"Ready to go?" Seth asked suddenly.

"Sure, if y–you are."

Holding the damaged dummy under one arm, Seth opened the shop door with his free hand. "I don't know about you, but I'm getting hungry. I think I can actually smell those fish-and-chips wafting up from the waterfront."

Tabby's mouth watered at the mention of eating succulent cod, deep-fried to perfection, and golden brown fries, dipped in tangy fry sauce. "Guess I'm kinda h–hungry too," she admitted.

Ten minutes later, they were parking in one of the huge lots near the waterfront. Seth reached for Tabby's hand as they crossed the street with the light.

Her hand tingled with his touch. *This does feel like a date,* she thought, though she didn't have a whole lot to gauge it on, considering she'd only been on a couple of dates since she graduated from high school. Those had been set up by Donna, and none of the guys had held her hand or acted the least bit interested in her. Of course, she hadn't said more than a few words, and those had come out in a mishmash of stammering and stuttering.

Groups of people were milling about the waterfront. Tabby clung tightly to Seth's hand, not wishing to get separated. As they headed down the sidewalk toward one of the fish bars, she spotted a young man walking a few feet ahead of them. He had two sizable holes in the back of his faded blue jeans, and long, scraggly brown hair hung halfway down the back of his discolored orange T-shirt. That was not what drew her attention to him, however. What made this man so unique was the colorful parrot sitting on his shoulder. With each step the man took, the parrot would either let out an ear-piercing squawk or imitate something someone had just said.

"I'm hungry! I'm hungry!" the feathered creature screeched. "The ferry's coming! The ferry's coming! Awk!"

Tabby glanced to her left. Sure enough, the Vashon Island ferry was heading toward one of the piers. Enthusiastic children jumped up and down, hollering that the ferry was coming, and the noisy parrot kept right on mimicking.

"I don't know who's more interesting—that guy with the long hair or his obnoxious bird," Seth whispered to Tabby.

She giggled. "The b–bird has my vote."

"I heard this story about a guy who owned a belligerent parrot," Seth remarked.

She looked up at him expectantly. "And?"

"The parrot had a bad attitude, not to mention a very foul mouth."

"So, what h–happened?"

"The guy tried everything from playing soft music to saying only polite words in front of the bird, but nothing worked at all."

"Did he s–sell the parrot then?"

Seth shook his head. "Nope. He put him in the freezer."

Tabby's mouth dropped open. "The freezer?"

"Yep, for about five minutes. When he opened the door again, the parrot calmly stepped out onto the guy's shoulder, a changed bird."

"He didn't use b–bad words anymore?"

"Nope. In fact, the parrot said, 'I'm truly sorry for being so rude.' Then the colorful creature added, 'Say, I saw a naked chicken in that icebox. What'd that poor bird do?' "

Tabby laughed, feeling happy and carefree, and wishing the fun of today could last forever.

Seth sobered, nodding toward the edge of the sidewalk. "You see all kinds down here."

Tabby watched with interest as a group of peddlers offered their wares to anyone who would listen. Everything from costume jewelry to painted T-shirts was being sold. Several men lay on the grass, holding signs announcing that they were out of work and needed money. An empty coffee can sat nearby—a place for donations. Tabby thought it sad to see people who were homeless or out of a job, reduced to begging. These few along the waterfront were just the tip of the iceberg too.

"It's hard to distinguish between who really needs help and who's merely panhandling," Seth whispered in her ear.

She nodded, wondering if he could read her mind.

"Ivar's has a long line of people waiting to get in," Seth said. "Is it okay with you if we try Steamer's Fish Bar instead?"

Tabby glanced at the restaurant he'd mentioned. The aroma of deep-fried fish drifted out the open door and filled up her senses. "One fish-and-chips place is probably as good as another," she replied.

They entered the restaurant and placed their orders at the counter, then found a seat near a window overlooking the water. Tabby watched in fascination as several boats pulled away from the dock, taking tourists on a journey through Puget Sound Bay. It was a beautiful, sunny day—perfect weather for boating.

"Would you like to go?"

Seth's sudden question drew Tabby's attention away from the window. "G–go? But we j–just got here," she said frowning.

Seth grinned. "I didn't mean go home. I meant, would you like to go for a ride on one of those tour boats you're watching so intently? We could do that after we eat, instead of browsing through the gift shops."

"Do w–we have t–time for th–that?"

Seth glanced at his watch. "I don't see why not. My shop's closed for the day, and I don't have to be back at any set time. How about you?"

Tabby shook her head. "I have all d–day."

"Then would you like me to see about getting a couple of tour-boat tickets?"

Tabby felt the tension begin to seep from her body as she reached for her glass of lemonade. "Actually, if I h–had a choice, I think I'd r–rather take the ferry over to V–Vashon, then ferry from there b–back to Tacoma."

Seth's face brightened. "Now that's a great idea! I haven't ridden the ferry in quite awhile."

❧

Tabby hung tightly to the rail as she leaned over to stare into the choppy waters of Puget Sound Bay. The wind whipped against her face, slapping the ends of her hair in every direction. It was exhilarating, and she felt very much alive. Seagulls soared in the cloudless sky, squawking and screeching, as though vying for the attention of everyone on board the ferry. It was a peaceful scene, and Tabby felt a deep sense of contentment fill her soul.

Seth was standing directly behind Tabby, and he leaned into her, wrapping his arms around her waist. "Warm enough?" he asked, his mouth pressed against her ear.

Tabby shivered, and she knew it was not from the cool breeze. "I'm fine."

Seth rested his chin on top of her head. "This was a great idea. I've had a lot of fun today."

"Me too," she murmured.

"It doesn't have to end when we dock at Point Defiance."

"It doesn't?"

"Nope. We could have dinner at the Harbor Lights."

Tabby glanced down at her outfit and grimaced. "I'm not exactly dressed for a fancy restaurant, Seth."

He chuckled. "Me neither, but I don't think it matters much. A lot of boaters pull into the docks at the restaurants along Tacoma's waterfront. I'm sure many people will be dressed as casually as we are."

Tabby shrugged. She was having such a good time and didn't want the day to end yet. "Okay. . .if you're sure."

"I'm positive," Seth said, nuzzling her neck.

She sucked in her breath. If this was a dream, she hoped it would last forever.

❧

Seth sat directly across from Tabby, studying her instead of the menu he held in his hands. She was gazing intently at her own menu, which gave him the perfect opportunity to look at her without being noticed. When had she taken on such a glow? When had her eyes begun to sparkle? He shook his head. Maybe it was just the reflection from the candle in the center of the table. Maybe he was imagining things.

Tabby looked up and caught him staring. "What's wrong?" she asked with furrowed brows. "Don't you see anything you like?"

Seth's lips curved into a slow smile.

"What's so funny?"

He reached across the table and grasped her hand. "Two things are making me smile."

She gave him a quizzical look.

"You haven't stuttered once since we left Seattle."

Tabby's face turned crimson, making Seth wonder if he should have said anything. "I didn't mean to embarrass you. It makes me happy to know you're finally beginning to relax in my presence."

She returned his smile. "I do feel pretty calm tonight."

He ran his thumb across the top of her hand and felt relief when she didn't pull it away.

"You said there were two things making you smile. What's the second one?"

He leaned further across the table. "Just looking at you makes me smile."

A tiny frown marred her forehead. "Am I that goofy looking?"

Seth shook his head. "No, of course not! In fact, I was sitting here thinking how beautiful you look in the candlelight."

"No one has ever c–called me b–beautiful before," she said, a blush staining her cheeks.

Great! Now she's stuttering again. So much for making her feel relaxed. Seth dropped her hand and picked up his menu. "Guess I'd better decide what to order before our waiter comes back. Have you found anything you like yet?"

Tabby nodded. "I think I'll have a crab salad."

"You can order whatever you want," Seth said quickly. "Lobster, steak, or prime rib—just say the word."

"Crab salad is all I want," she insisted.

Seth was about to comment when the waiter returned to their table.

"Have you two decided?" the young man asked.

"I'll have prime rib, and the lady wants a crab salad." Seth handed both menus back to the waiter. "I think we'll have two glasses of iced tea as well."

As soon as the waiter left, Seth reached for Tabby's hand again. "I didn't mean to make you blush a few minutes ago. How come you always do that, anyway?"

"Do what?"

"Turn red like a cherry and hang your head whenever you're paid a compliment."

Her forehead wrinkled. "I–I don't know. I'm not used to getting compliments. You don't have to try and make me feel good, you know."

"Is that what you think—that I'm just trying to make you feel good?"

"Well, isn't it?"

His throat tightened. "I don't pass out false compliments so someone will feel good, Tabby."

Her gaze dropped to the tablecloth. "Let's forget it, okay?"

Seth offered up a silent prayer. *Should I let this drop, Lord, or should I try to convince her that I'm really interested in her as a woman, and that. . .* He swallowed hard. What did he really want from this relationship? When he'd first met Tabby, he'd felt sorry for her. He could sense her need for encouragement and maybe even a friend, but when had he started thinking of her as a woman and not just someone to help? There was a great yearning, deep within him, and he wondered if it could be filled by a woman's love. Tabby might be that woman. He had thought about her nearly every day since they first met. That had to mean something, didn't it?

Seth felt a sense of peace settle over him as he heard the words in his head say, *Go slow, Seth. Go slow.*

twelve

"I can't believe you were gone all day!" Donna exclaimed when Tabby entered their apartment.

Tabby dropped to the couch beside her and released a sigh of contentment. "Today was probably the best day of my life."

Donna's eyebrows shot up. "Did Seth kiss you?"

"Of course not!"

"You're turning red like a radish. He must have kissed you." Donna poked Tabby in the ribs. "Tell me all about it, and don't leave out one single detail."

Tabby slid out of Donna's reach. "Don't get so excited. There's not that much to tell."

"Then start with when Seth picked you up this morning and end with a detailed description of his kiss."

Tabby grimaced. "I told you, there was no kiss!" Her inexperience with men was an embarrassment. If she'd been more coy, like that cute little redhead, Cheryl, maybe Seth would have kissed her.

"Then what has you glowing like a Christmas tree?" Donna asked, pulling Tabby out of her musings.

"Seth is a lot of fun, and I had a good time today," she mumbled.

Donna released a sigh. "That sure doesn't tell me much."

Tabby leaned her head against the back of the couch. "Let's see. . . We drove to Seattle, and freeway traffic was terrible." A long pause followed.

"And?"

"When we got to Seattle, we went to the Dummy Depot to

pick up a ventriloquist figure Seth needs to repair." Another long pause.

"Then what?"

"We went down to the waterfront, where we had a great lunch of fish-and-chips."

"You must have done more than that. You've been gone all day."

Tabby glanced at her watch and wrinkled her nose. "It's only a little after eight. Besides, you're not my mother, and I'm not on any kind of a curfew."

Donna squinted her eyes. "You look like you're on cloud nine, so I figure you must have done something really exciting today."

Tabby grinned. "We did. We rode the ferry from Seattle to Vashon Island, then we caught another one to Point Defiance." She closed her eyes and thought about Seth's arms around her waist and his mouth pressed against her ear. She could still feel his warm breath on her neck and smell his woodsy aftershave lotion. That part of the day had been the most exciting thing of all. She wasn't about to share such a private moment with Donna—even if she was her best friend.

"What'd you do after you left Point Defiance?" Donna asked.

"We went to dinner at the Harbor Lights."

Donna let out a low whistle. "Wow! Things must be getting pretty serious between you two. The Harbor Lights costs big bucks!"

Tabby groaned. "It's not that expensive. Besides, going there doesn't mean anything special."

Donna gave her a knowing look. "Yeah, right."

"It's true," Tabby insisted. "I'm the queen of simplicity, so why would a great guy like Seth be attracted to someone like me?"

Donna clicked her tongue. "Are you ever going to see your true potential?"

Crossing her arms in front of her chest, Tabby shrugged. "I don't know. Maybe I do have some worth."

❧

After their day in Seattle, Tabby had hoped Seth might call and ask her out again. That would have let her know if he really was interested in seeing her on a personal level or not. However, the week went by without a single word from him. Today was Thursday, and she had another, previously scheduled ventriloquism lesson that evening. Thinking about it had very little appeal, though. If only Seth had called. If only. . .

As she drove across town, Tabby forced her thoughts away from Seth and onto the routine she'd been practicing with Rosie. She was determined to do her very best this time. Even if Seth never saw her as a desirable woman, at least she could dazzle the socks off him with her new talent.

When she arrived at Seth's, Tabby was relieved to see he had no customers. The thought of performing before an audience held no appeal whatsoever.

Seth greeted her with a warm smile. "I'll be with you in just a minute. I have to make a few phone calls."

Tabby nodded and took a seat, placing Rosie on her lap. Mentally, she began to rehearse the lines of her routine, hoping she had them memorized so well she wouldn't have to use her notes. Watching Seth as he stood across the room talking on the phone was a big enough distraction, but when the bell above the shop door rang, announcing a customer, Tabby froze.

In walked Cheryl Stone carrying her dummy, Oscar. She hurried past Tabby as though she hadn't even seen her and rushed up to Seth just as he was hanging up the phone. "Seth, you've got to help me!" she exclaimed.

"What do you need help with?" Seth asked.

"Oscar's mouth is stuck in the open position, and I can't get it to work." Cheryl handed him the dummy. "I'm supposed to do a vent routine at a family gathering tonight, and I was hoping you'd have time to fix Oscar for me."

Seth glanced at Tabby. "Actually, I was just about to begin teaching a lesson. Why don't you use your new dummy tonight—the one you recently bought from me?"

Cheryl shook her head. "I haven't gotten used to that one yet. Besides, Oscar's so cute, he's always a hit wherever I perform."

"Have a seat then," Seth said, motioning toward the row of chairs along the wall where Tabby sat. "I'll take Oscar in the back room and see what I can do."

Cheryl smiled sweetly. "Thank you, Seth. You're the nicest man."

The chocolate bar Tabby had eaten on her drive over to Seth's suddenly felt like a lump of clay in her stomach. Cheryl obviously had her eye on Seth. For all Tabby knew, he might have more than a passing interest in the vibrant redhead too.

Cheryl took a seat next to Tabby, opened her purse, withdrew a nail file, and began to shape her nails. The silence closing in around them was broken only by the steady ticking of the wall clock across the room and the irritating scrape of nail file against fingernails.

Should I say something to her? Tabby wondered. Just sitting here like this felt so awkward. Given her problem with stuttering, she decided that unless Cheryl spoke first, she would remain quiet.

Several minutes went by, and then Cheryl returned the nail file to her purse and turned toward Tabby. "Cute little dummy you've got there."

"Th–thanks."

"Are you here to see about getting it repaired?"

Tabby shook her head. "I–I'm t–taking l–lessons." She glanced toward the back room, hoping Seth would return soon. There was something about Cheryl's confidence and good looks that shattered any hope Tabby might have of ever becoming a successful ventriloquist, much less the object of Seth's affections.

Cheryl tapped her fingers along the arm of the chair. "I wonder what's taking so long? Seth must be having quite a time with Oscar's stubborn little mouth." She eyed Tabby curiously. "How long have you been taking ventriloquism lessons?"

"Not l–long."

"Guess you'll be at it for awhile, what with your stuttering problem and all." Cheryl offered Tabby a sympathetic smile. "It must be difficult for you."

Hot tears stung Tabby's eyes as she squirmed in her seat, then hunkered down as if succumbing to a predator. She bit her lower lip to stop the flow of tears that seemed insistent on spilling onto her flaming cheeks. She was used to her family making fun of her speech impediment, but seeing the pity on Cheryl's face was almost worse than reproach.

Dear Lord, she prayed silently, *please help me say something without stuttering.*

With newfound courage, Tabby stuck her hand into the opening at the back of Rosie's overalls, grabbed the control stick, opened her own mouth slightly, and said in a falsetto voice, "Tabby may have a problem with shyness, but I don't stutter at all." It was true, Tabby noted with satisfaction. Whenever she did ventriloquism, the voice she used for her dummy never missed a syllable.

Cheryl leaned forward, squinting her eyes and watching intently as Tabby continued to make her dummy talk.

"My name's Rosie; what's yours?"

"Cheryl Stone, and my dummy, Oscar, is in there getting his mouth worked on." Cheryl pointed toward the room where Seth had disappeared.

Tabby smiled. She could hardly believe it, but Cheryl was actually talking to her dummy like it was real. Of course,

Cheryl was a ventriloquist, and people who talked for two did seem to have the childlike ability to get into the whole dummy scene.

"How long have you been doing ventriloquism?" little Rosie asked Cheryl.

Cheryl smiled in response. "I learned the basics on my own a few years ago. Since I met Seth, he's taught me several advanced techniques."

I wonder what else he's taught you. Tabby opened Rosie's mouth, actually planning to voice the question, but Seth entered the room in the nick of time.

"I think Oscar's good to go," he said, handing the dummy to Cheryl.

Cheryl jumped up. "How can I ever thank you, Seth?" She stood on tiptoes and planted a kiss right on Seth's lips!

Tabby wasn't sure who was more surprised—she or Seth. He stood there for several seconds, face red and mouth hanging open. Finally, he grinned, embarrassed-like, then mumbled, "I'll send you a bill."

Cheryl giggled and gave his arm a squeeze. "You're so cute." As started for the door, she called over her shoulder, "See you on Saturday, Seth!" The door clicked shut, and Cheryl Stone was gone.

Tabby wished she had the courage to ask Seth why he'd be seeing Cheryl on Saturday, but it didn't seem appropriate. Besides, she had no claim on him, and if he chose to date someone else, who was she to ask questions?

"Sorry about the interruption," Seth said in a business-like tone of voice. "We can begin now, if you're ready."

Tabby swallowed hard. Cheryl was gone, but the image of her lovely face rolled around in Tabby's mind. She'd been more than ready for a lesson when she came into Seth's shop, but now, after seeing the interchange between Seth and Cheryl, the only thing she was ready for was home!

thirteen

Seth eased into a chair and leaned forward until his head was resting in his hands. He couldn't believe how terrible Tabby's lesson had gone. Beside the fact that there had been an air of tension between them ever since Cheryl left, Tabby seemed unable to stay focused. What had gone wrong? Was he failing as a teacher, or was she simply losing interest in ventriloquism? Did she have any personal feelings for him, or had he read more into their Seattle trip than there actually was? Tabby seemed so relaxed that day, and when he'd held her hand, she hadn't pulled away. In fact, as near as he could tell, she'd enjoyed it as much as he had.

Seth groaned and stood up again. He wasn't sure how or even when it happened, but Tabitha Johnson definitely meant more to him than just someone to help. After seeing the way she was with her day care kids the other day, and after spending time with her in Seattle, he really was beginning to hope she was the woman he'd been waiting for. If he could only make Tabby see what potential she had. If she could just get past all that shyness and stuttering, he was sure she'd be perfect for him.

He moved toward the telephone. Tabby wouldn't be home yet. Maybe it was time for that talk with her friend.

Donna answered on the second ring. Seth quickly related the reason for his call, and a few minutes later he hung up the phone, happy in the knowledge that he'd be meeting Donna for lunch tomorrow. Between the two of them, maybe Tabby could become a confident woman who would use all her abilities to serve the Lord.

"I am so glad this is Friday," Tabby murmured, as she prepared to eat her sack lunch at one of the small tables where the day care kids often sat.

"Me too," Donna agreed. She grabbed her sweater and umbrella and started for the door. "See you later."

"Hey, wait a minute," Tabby called. "Where are you going?"

"Out to lunch, and I'd better hurry."

"Say, why don't I join you?"

"See you at one." Donna waved and disappeared out the door before Tabby could say another word and without even answering her question.

Tabby's forehead wrinkled. Donna hardly ever went out to lunch on a weekday. When she did, she always arranged for one of their helpers to take over the day care so Tabby could come along. What was up, anyway?

Tabby snapped her fingers. "Maybe Donna has a date and doesn't want me to know about it. I'll bet there's a mystery man in my friend's life."

"Who are you talking to, Teacher?"

Tabby jerked her head at the sound of four-year-old Mary Steven's sweet voice.

"I—uh—was kind of talking to myself."

Mary grinned. "Like you do when you use Roscoe or little Rosie?"

Tabby nodded. "Something like that." She patted the child on top of her curly, blond head. "What are you doing up, Missy? It's nap time, you know."

The child nodded soberly. "I'm not sleepy."

"Maybe not, but you need to rest your eyes." Tabby placed her ham sandwich back inside its plastic wrapper and stood up. "Come on, Sweetie, I'll walk you back to your sleeping mat."

❧

Seth tapped the edge of his water glass with the tip of his spoon, as he waited impatiently for Donna to show up. She'd promised to meet him at Garrison's Deli shortly after noon. It was only a few doors down from the church where she and Tabby ran their day care center. It shouldn't take her more than a few minutes to get here.

He glanced at his watch again. Twelve-twenty. Where was she anyway? Maybe she'd forgotten. Maybe she'd changed her mind. He was just about to leave the table and go to the counter to place his order, when he saw Donna come rushing into the deli.

She waved, then hurried toward his table. Her face was flushed, and her dark curls looked windblown. "Sorry I'm late," she panted. "Just as I was leaving the day care, Tabby started plying me with all sorts of questions about where I was having lunch, and she even suggested she come along. I chose to ignore her and hurried out of the room. Then I got detained a few more minutes on my way out of the church."

Seth gave her a questioning look as she took the seat directly across from him.

"One of the kids' parents came to pick him up early. She stopped me on the steps to say Bobby had a dental appointment and she'd forgotten to tell us about it," Donna explained.

Seth nodded toward the counter. "I was about to order. Do you know what you want, or do you need a few minutes to look at the menu?"

"Chicken salad in pita bread and a glass of iced tea sounds good to me," she replied.

"I'll be right back," Seth said, pushing away from the table. He placed Donna's order first, then ordered a turkey club sandwich on whole wheat with a glass of apple juice for himself. When he returned to the table, he found Donna staring out the window.

"Looks like it could rain again," he noted.

She held up the umbrella she'd placed on one end of the table. "I came prepared."

Seth decided there was no point in wasting time talking about the weather. "I was wondering if we could discuss Tabby," he blurted out. "That day you came into my shop to get the gift certificate for Tabby's dummy, we agreed that we'd work together to help her. I've really been trying, but to tell you the truth, I kind of feel like a salmon swimming upstream."

Donna giggled. "How can I help?"

"I have a few questions for you," he answered.

"What do you want to know?"

"I've never met anyone quite as shy as Tabby," he said. "Can you tell me why that is and what makes her stutter?"

Donna drew in a deep breath and exhaled it with such force that her napkin blew off the table. "Whew. . .that's kind of a long story." She bent down to retrieve the napkin, then glanced at her watch. "This will have to be a scaled down version, because I have to be back at work by one."

Seth leaned forward with his elbows on the table. "I'm all ears."

"I've known Tabby ever since we were little tykes," Donna began. "Up until she turned six, Tabby was a fun-loving, outgoing child."

"What happened when she turned six?"

"Her sister was born." Donna grimaced. "Tabby's dad favored Lois right from the start. I can't explain why, but he started giving Tabby putdowns and harsh words. She turned inward, became introverted, and began to lack confidence in most areas of her life." She drummed her fingers along the edge of the table. "That's when she began stuttering."

Seth was about to reply, but their order was being called. He excused himself to pick up their food. When he returned to the table, Seth offered a word of prayer, and they both grabbed their sandwiches. "Do you think you can eat and talk at the same time?" he asked.

"Oh, sure, I've had lots of practice," Donna mumbled around her pita bread.

"I've noticed that Tabby stutters more at certain times, and other times she hardly stutters at all."

Donna nodded. "It has to do with how well she knows you, and how comfortable she feels in your presence."

"So, if Tabby felt more confident and had more self-esteem, she probably wouldn't stutter as much—or at all."

Donna shrugged. "Could be. Tabby's worst stuttering takes place when she's around her family. They intimidate her, and she's never learned to stand up for herself."

Seth took a swallow of apple juice, and his eyebrows furrowed. "Tabby doesn't stutter at all when she does ventriloquism. It's almost like she's a different person when she's speaking through her dummy."

Donna shrugged. "In a way, I guess she is."

"Just when I think I've got her figured out, she does something to muddle my brain."

"Like what?"

"Last night was a good example," Seth answered. "Tabby arrived at my shop for another lesson, and I thought she was in a good mood, ready to learn and all excited about it."

"She was excited," Donna agreed. "She's been enthusiastic about everything since the two of you went to Seattle."

Seth brightened some. "Really? I thought she'd had a good time, but I wasn't sure."

Donna grinned. "Tabby was on cloud nine when she came home that night." Her hand went quickly to her mouth. "Oops. . . Guess I wasn't supposed to tell you that."

Seth felt his face flush. That was the trouble with being fair skinned and redheaded. He flushed way too easily. *Tabby must have some feelings for me. At least she did until. . .*

"Tell me what happened last night to make you wonder about Tabby," Donna said, interrupting his thoughts.

He took a bite of his sandwich, then washed it down with more juice before answering. "As I said before, Tabby was in a good mood when she first came in."

"And?"

"Then an unexpected customer showed up, and after she left, Tabby closed up like a razor clam."

"Hmm. . ."

"Hmm. . .what?"

Donna frowned. "Tabby was in kind of a sour mood when she came home last night. I asked her what was wrong, and she mumbled something about not being able to compete with Cheryl." She eyed Seth speculatively. "Cheryl wouldn't happen to be that unexpected customer, would she?"

"Afraid so. Cheryl Stone is a confident young woman with lots of talent as a ventriloquist."

"Is she pretty?"

He nodded. Cheryl was beautiful, vivacious, and talented. *That perfect woman you've been looking for,* a little voice taunted. *If Cheryl is perfect, then why do I think I need to remake Tabby?*

"Will you be seeing Tabby again?" Donna asked.

He swallowed hard, searching for the right words. Did he love her? Did she love him? He enjoyed being with her, that much he knew. Was it love he was feeling, though? It was probably too soon to tell.

"I–I don't know if we'll see each other again," he finally answered. "Guess that all depends on Tabby."

"On whether she wants more lessons?" Donna pried.

Seth shrugged. "That and a few other things."

Donna didn't pry, and he was glad. He wasn't in the mood to try and explain his feelings for Tabitha Johnson, or this compelling need he felt to make her into the woman he thought he needed.

"Well," Donna said a few minutes later, "I really do need

to get back to work." She finished her iced tea and stood up. "Thanks for lunch, Seth. I hope some of the things we've talked about have been helpful. Tabby's my best friend, and I care a lot about her." She looked at him pointedly. "She carries a lot of pain from the past. I don't want to see her hurt anymore."

Seth stood up too. "My car's parked right out front. I'll walk you out," he said, making no reference to the possibility that he might add further hurt to Tabby's already battered mental state. He was so confused about everything right now, and some things were better left unsaid. Especially when he hadn't fully sorted out his feelings for her and didn't have a clue how she really felt about him.

≈

With a bag of trash in her arms, Tabby left Gail, their eighteen-year-old helper, in charge of the day care kids while she carried the garbage out to the curb. The garbage truck always came around three on Friday afternoons, which meant she still had enough time to get one more bag put out.

Tabby stepped up beside the two cans by the curb and had just opened the lid of one, when she heard voices coming from down the street. She turned her head to the right and froze in place, one hand holding the garbage can lid, the other clutching the plastic garbage bag.

She could see a man and woman standing outside Garrison's Deli. She'd have recognized them anywhere—Seth for his red hair; Donna for her high-pitched laugh. What were they doing together? Tabby's mouth dropped open like a broken hinge on a screen door. Her body began to sway. She blinked rapidly, hoping her eyes had deceived her. Seth was actually hugging her best friend!

fourteen

Tabby dropped the garbage sack into the can, slammed the lid down, whirled around, and bolted for the church. She didn't want Donna or Seth to see her. She had to think. . .to decide the best way to handle this little matter. Would it be better to come right out and ask Donna what she was doing with Seth, or should she merely ply her with a few questions, hoping the answers would come voluntarily?

Tabby returned to the day care center with a heavy heart. Were Seth and Donna seeing each other socially? Was he Donna's lunch date? Was he the mystery man in her best friend's life? As much as the truth might hurt, she had to know.

Tabby was setting out small tubs of modeling clay when Donna sauntered into the room humming "Jesus Loves Me." She looked about as blissful as a kitten with a ball of string, and not the least bit guilty, either.

"How was lunch?" Tabby asked after Donna had put her purse and umbrella in the desk drawer.

"It was good. I had pita bread stuffed with chicken salad."

"What did your date have?"

Donna spun around, and her eyebrows shot up. "My date?"

"Yeah, the person you met for lunch."

"Did I say I was meeting someone?"

Tabby shrugged. "Not in so many words, but you acted kind of secretive. Are you seeing some guy you don't want me to know about?"

Donna lowered herself into one of the kiddy chairs, keeping her eyes averted from Tabby's penetrating gaze. "Let's just say I'm checking him out. I need to see how well we get along. I want to find out what he's really like."

Tabby opened one of the clay lids and slapped it down on the table. "Why didn't you just ask me? I know exactly what he's like!"

Donna's forehead wrinkled, and she pursed her lips. "Since when do you have the inside scoop on our pastor's son?"

"Who?"

"Alex Hanson."

"Alex? What's Alex got to do with this?"

"I had lunch with Alex the Saturday you and Seth went to Seattle," Donna explained.

Tabby's insides began to quiver. What was going on here, anyway? "That's fine. I'm happy you finally agreed to go out with Alex, but what about today? Did you or did you not have lunch with someone over at Garrison's Deli?"

Donna's face grew red, and little beads of perspiration gathered on her forehead. "Well, I—"

"You don't have to hem and haw or beat around the bush with me," Tabby grunted. "I know perfectly well who you had lunch with today."

"You do?"

Tabby nodded. "I took some garbage outside a little while ago. I heard voices, and when I looked down the street, there stood Seth—with his arms around my best friend!" She flopped into a chair and buried her face in her hands.

Donna reached over and laid a hand on Tabby's trembling shoulder, but Tabby jerked it away. "How could you go behind my back like that?"

"You're wrong. Things aren't the way they appear."

Tabby snapped her head up. "Are you going to deny having had lunch with Seth?"

"No, but—"

"Was it you and Seth standing in front of the deli?"

"Yes, but—"

"You can't argue the fact that he was hugging you, either, can you?"

Donna shook her head. "No, I can't deny any of those things, but I'm not the least bit interested in Seth. We've been through all this before, Tabby, and—"

"Just how do you explain the secret lunch. . .or that tender little embrace?"

Donna's eyes filled with tears. "I didn't want you to know I was meeting Seth, because I didn't want you to think we were ganging up on you."

Tabby bit her bottom lip, sucking it inside her mouth when she tasted blood. "In what way are you ganging up on me?"

"Can't we talk about this later? The kids will be up from their naps soon," Donna said, glancing toward the adjoining room.

Tabby lifted her arm, then held it so her watch was a few inches from Donna's face. "We still have three minutes. I think you can answer my question in that amount of time, don't you?"

Donna pulled a tissue from her skirt pocket and blew her nose. "Guess you don't leave me much choice."

Tabby's only response was a curt nod.

"It's like this. . .Seth was concerned about your actions last night. He said you didn't do well at your lesson, and that you seemed kinda remote. He's trying hard to help you overcome your shyness, and perfect your—"

"So the two of you are in cahoots, trying to fix poor, pitiful, timid Tabitha!" Tabby shouted. She could feel the pulse hammering in her neck, and her hands had begun to shake.

Donna's eyelids fluttered. "Calm down. You'll wake the kids."

Tabby pointed to her watch. "It's almost time for them to get up anyway."

"That may be true, but you don't want to scare the little

tykes with your screeching, do you?"

Tabby sniffed deeply. "Of course not. But I'm really upset right now, and I'm not sure who I should be angrier with—you or Seth."

Donna grimaced. "Sorry. I didn't mean to get you all riled up. I just thought—"

Donna's sentence was interrupted when a group of children came trooping into the room, chattering and giggling all the way to the table.

Donna gave Tabby a look. For now, this conversation was over.

੨৯

Seth hung up the phone, wondering why he'd ever agreed to recruit another ventriloquist to perform with him at the Clearview Church Family Crusade. The female ventriloquist who'd originally been scheduled to perform had just canceled out. Now they were asking him to find a replacement.

Seth knew plenty of ventriloquists. The trouble was, it was so last minute. The crusade was set for next Friday night, and finding someone at this late date would be next to impossible. If only he could come up with. . .

The bell above his shop door rang sharply as a customer entered the shop. It was almost closing time, and the last thing Seth needed was one more problem he didn't know how to fix. He glanced up, and his heart seemed as though it had quit beating. It was Tabby, and she didn't look any too happy.

"Hi," Seth said cheerfully. "I'm glad to see you. You never called about having another lesson, and—"

Tabby held up one hand. "I've decided I don't need any more lessons."

"Then why are you here? You're not having a problem with Rosie, I hope."

She shook her head. "No, I w–wanted to talk about—"

Seth snapped his fingers, cutting her off in mid-sentence.

"Say, you just might be the answer to my prayers!"

She furrowed her brows and turned her hands, palm up. "I d–don't get it."

He motioned toward a folding chair. "Have a seat, and I'll tell you about it."

When Tabby sat down, Seth took the chair next to her.

"Well, h–how am I an answer t–to your prayers?" she asked.

He reached for her hand. This was not going to be easy. Only a God-given miracle would make Tabby willing to do what he asked.

&

Tabby was tempted to pull her hand from Seth's, but she didn't. It felt good. In fact, she wished she'd never have to let go. She stared up at him, searching his face for answers.

"I—uh—will be doing a vent routine at Clearview Community Church next Friday night," Seth began slowly.

"What's that got to do with me?"

"I'm getting to that." He smiled sheepishly. "The thing is, Sarah McDonald, the other ventriloquist who was originally scheduled, has had a family emergency and was forced to bow out." Seth ran his thumb along the inside of Tabby's palm, making it that much harder for her to concentrate on what he was saying. "I was hoping you might be willing to go with me next week—to fill in for Sarah."

Tabby's throat constricted, and she drew in a deep, unsteady breath. Did Seth actually think she could stand up in front of an audience and talk for two? He should be smart enough to realize she wasn't ready for something like that. The truth was, even though she had gained a bit more confidence, she might never be able to do ventriloquism for a large audience.

"I know it's short notice," Seth said, jerking her thoughts aside, "but we could begin practicing right now, then do more throughout the week. I'm sure—"

The rest of Seth's sentence was lost, as Tabby closed her eyes and tried to imagine what it would be like to perform before a crowd. She could visualize herself freezing up and not being able to utter a single word. Or worse yet, stuttering and stammering all over the place.

"Tabby, are you listening to me?" Seth's mellow voice pulled her out of the make-believe situation, and she popped her eyes open.

"I c–can't d–do it, Seth."

He pulled her to her feet, then placed both his hands on her shoulders. "You can do it, so don't be discouraged because you believe you have no ability. Each of us has much to offer. It's what you do with your abilities that really matters. Now, repeat after me. . .'I can do everything through him who gives me strength.'"

In a trembling voice, Tabby repeated the verse of Scripture from Philippians 4:13. When she was done, Seth tipped her chin up slightly, so they were making direct eye contact. "I know you can do this, Tabby."

She merely shrugged in response.

"You're a talented ventriloquist, and it's time to let your light shine," Seth said with feeling. He leaned his head down until his lips were mere inches from hers. "Do this for me, please."

Tabby's eyelids fluttered, then drifted shut. She felt the warmth of Seth's lips against her own. His kiss was gentle like a butterfly, but as intense as anything she'd ever felt. Of course, her inexperience in the kissing department didn't offer much for comparison. Tabby knew she was falling for Seth Beyers, and she wanted desperately to please him. She'd come over here this evening to give him a piece of her mind, but now all such thoughts had melted away, like spring's last snow. She reveled in the joy of being held in Seth's arms and delighted in the warmth of his lips caressing her own.

When they pulled apart moments later, Tabby felt as if all the breath had been squeezed out of her lungs.

"Kissing is good for you, did you know that?" Seth murmured against her ear.

Numbly she shook her head.

"Yep. It helps relieve stress and tension. Just think about it—when your mouth is kissing, you're almost smiling. Everyone knows it's impossible to smile and feel tense at the same time."

Tabby leaned her head against his shoulder. She did feel relaxed, happy, and almost confident. In a voice sounding much like her dummy's, she rasped, "Okay, I'll do it. Rosie and I will p–perform a vent routine."

He grinned and clasped his hands together. "Great! I know you'll be perfect."

fifteen

Tabby awoke the following morning wondering if she'd completely lost her mind. What in the world had come over her last night? Not only had she not told Seth what she thought about him trying to change her, but she'd actually agreed to do a vent routine next week—in front of a large audience, no less!

"It was that kiss," Tabby moaned as she threw back the covers and crawled out of bed. "If only he hadn't kissed me, I could have said no."

She winced, as though she'd been slapped. Would she really rather he hadn't kissed her? In all honesty, if Seth would offer another of his sweet kisses, she'd probably say yes all over again.

Feeling more like a dummy than a ventriloquist, Tabby padded in her bare feet over to the window and peered through the mini-blinds. The sun was shining. The birds were singing. It was going to be a beautiful day. Too bad her heart felt no joy. She turned and headed for the kitchen, feeling as though she was part of a death march.

Discovering Donna sitting at the table, talking on the cordless phone, Tabby dropped into a chair. When Donna offered her a warm smile, she only grunted in response.

By the time Donna's conversation was over, Tabby had eaten an orange, along with a handful of grapes, and she was about to tackle a banana. "Good morning, Sleepyhead. I thought you were never going to get up."

"I got in late last night," Tabby mumbled as she bit into the piece of fruit.

"Tell me about it!" Donna exclaimed. "I finally gave up waiting for you and went to bed. You said you had an errand to run after work. Where were you anyway?"

Tabby swallowed the chunk of banana and frowned. "I'm afraid my errand turned into more of an error."

Donna's eyebrows lifted in question.

"I went to Beyers' Ventriloquist Studio, planning to put Seth in his place for trying to run my life."

"And did you?"

Tabby sucked in her bottom lip and squared her shoulders. "Afraid not. I ended up promising to do a vent routine at the Clearview Church Family Crusade next Friday."

Donna slapped her hand down on the table, and Tabby's banana peel flew into the air, landing on the floor. "Awesome! That's the best news I've had all year. Maybe even in the last ten years!"

Tabby shook her head. "Don't get so excited. I haven't done it yet."

"Oh, but you will," Donna said excitedly. She pointed to the phone. "That call was from Alex Hanson. He asked me to go out with him again, and guess where we're going?"

"Please don't tell me it's the crusade," Tabby said, already knowing the answer.

"Okay, I won't tell you. I'll just let you be surprised when you look out into the audience and see your best friend and your pastor's son cheering you on."

Tabby gazed at the ceiling. "I think I need a doctor to examine my head more than I need a cheering section." She groaned. "I can't believe I let Seth talk me into such a thing!"

"You'll do just fine," Donna said with an assurance Tabby sure didn't feel. "I imagine you and Seth did some practicing last night?"

Yeah, that and a few other things. Tabby wasn't about to discuss Seth's kiss. Donna would probably go ballistic if she knew that had happened. "We had a bite of supper at the café near Seth's shop, then we worked on my routine 'til almost midnight." Tabby grimaced. "I'm lucky I even have any voice left after all that talking. Maybe I could get out of this if I had laryngitis or something. Seth asked me to do him a favor by filling in for someone else, and—"

"And you love the guy so much, you couldn't say no," Donna said, finishing Tabby's sentence.

Tabby's eyes filled with tears. "He wants me to be something I'm not."

"Which is?"

"Confident, talented, and ready to serve the Lord."

Donna reached across the table and patted Tabby's hand. "I've seen you do ventriloquism, so I know how talented you are. I also know you want to serve the Lord."

Tabby nodded and swiped at her face with the backs of her hands.

"The confident part will come if you give yourself half a chance," Donna assured her. "If you wallow around in self-pity the rest of your life, you'll never realize your full potential."

Tabby released a shuddering breath. "I know you're right, but I still stutter when I'm nervous or with people I don't know well. How can I become truly confident when I can't even talk right?"

"Philippians 4:13: 'I can do everything through him who gives me strength,' " Donna reminded.

Tabby sniffed. "Seth quoted that same verse last night."

"See," Donna said with a smile. "The Lord wants you to lean on Him. If you keep your focus on Jesus and not the audience, I know you can do that routine next week."

Tabby smiled weakly. "I hope so." Her eyes filled with fresh tears. "I owe you an apology for the other day. We've been friends a long time, and I should have known you'd never try to make a play for Seth behind my back."

Donna nodded. "You're right; I wouldn't. And you are forgiven."

Tabby and Seth met every evening for the next week to practice their routines for the crusade. Not only was it helpful for Tabby to memorize her lines and work on her fear of talking for two in public, but it was an opportunity to spend more time with Seth. Sometimes, after they were done for the night, he'd take her out for pie and coffee, and a few times they just sat and talked. They were drawing closer, there was no doubt in Tabby's mind, but much to her disappointment, Seth hadn't tried to kiss her again. Maybe he thought it best to keep things on a strictly business basis, since they were preparing to do a program and shouldn't be playing the game of romance when they needed to be working.

As she entered the Clearview Community Church that Friday night, carrying Rosie in a small suitcase, Tabby's heart thumped so hard she was sure everyone around could hear it. The driving force that enabled her to make the trip across town was the fact that Seth was counting on her, and she didn't want to let him down.

She spotted Seth talking to a man in the foyer. When he noticed Tabby, he motioned her to come over.

"Tabby, I'd like you to meet Pastor Tom Fletcher," Seth said, placing his arm around her waist. "He's heading up the program tonight."

"It's nice to meet you," the pastor said, reaching out to shake her hand.

She nodded and forced a smile. "N–nice to m–meet you too."

"Seth was just telling me that you've graciously agreed to fill in for Sarah McDonald. I sure do appreciate this."

Tabby cringed, wishing she could tell Pastor Fletcher the truth—she wasn't graciously filling in. She'd been coerced by Seth's honeyed words and his heart-melting kiss.

"Tabby's new at ventriloquism," Seth said to the preacher. "She's got lots of talent, though. Doesn't move her lips at all."

Right now I wish my lips were glued shut, she fretted. *I wish Seth would quit bragging about me. It'll only make the pastor expect more than I'm able to give.*

"Why don't we go backstage now?" Seth suggested, giving Tabby a little nudge.

She let herself be led along, feeling like a sheep heading straight for the slaughterhouse. If she lived through this ordeal, she'd be eternally grateful. She caught sight of Donna and her blond-haired date as they were entering the sanctuary. Donna waved, and Alex gave her a "thumbs-up." She managed a weak smile, but the truth was, she felt like crying.

As though he could read her mind, Seth bent down and whispered, "Relax. You'll do fine."

"I wish everyone would quit telling me that."

Seth offered her a reassuring smile. "Do you realize that your last sentence was spoken without one bit of stuttering?"

She shook her head. Right at this moment she could barely remember what her last sentence had been about, much less focus on the fact that she hadn't stuttered.

Seth led her through a door, and a few minutes later they were in a small room with several other performers. Tabby recognized a few of them who'd been part of the demonstration for Christian workers at her own church a few months ago. There were Mark Taylor, the magician from Portland, Oregon, and Gail Stevens, the chalk artist from Seattle. Tabby knew Donna would be glad to see her. She'd probably be practicing her chalk art in earnest after tonight's performance. Slow-Joe the Clown was busy practicing his animal twisting skills, and some puppeteers were lining up to do their puppet skit. Tabby envied them. . .partly because they were going first and could get their routine over with, but mostly because they had the advantage of a puppet box to hide behind. If only she didn't have to face that crowd out there in the sanctuary!

"Now remember," Seth said, pulling Tabby aside, "I'll go out first and do my routine with Rudy; then you'll come out with Rosie, and we'll do a little bantering with our dummies. By then your confidence should be bolstered, so I'll just bow out, and you'll be on your own."

She looked up at him with pleading eyes. "That's the part that has me so worried, Seth. Couldn't you stay by my side the whole time?"

He shrugged. "I suppose I could, but I think the audience will appreciate your talent more if they see you perform solo."

Who cares if the audience appreciates my talent? I just want to get through this ordeal and live to tell about it. Tabby's heart fluttered like a frightened baby bird, and she fidgeted with the bow on Rosie's new pink dress. Donna would be glad to see she'd taken her advice and dressed the dummy up a bit.

Seth reached for her hand and squeezed it. "Your fingers feel like icicles, Tabby. Take a deep breath, and try to relax."

"That's easy enough for you to say," she muttered. "You're an old pro at this."

It seemed like no time at all that Seth was being announced by Pastor Fletcher. He grabbed Rudy and his stand, blew Tabby a kiss, and walked confidently onto the stage.

Tabby stood as close to the stage door as she could without being seen. She didn't want to miss her cue and end up embarrassing both Seth and herself. Seth was doing a bang-up job with his routine, but she was too nervous to appreciate any of it. All too soon, Seth announced her.

Holding Rosie with one hand and balancing the metal stand Seth had given her with the other, Tabby swallowed the panic rising in her throat and moved slowly across the stage. Applause sounded from the audience, and she felt her face flame.

"Rudy and I both needed dates for tonight," Seth told the crowd. "This is my friend, Tabitha Johnson, and I'll let her introduce her little pal."

Tabby opened her mouth, but nothing came out. She just stood there, feeling like some kind of frozen snow woman, unable to remember her lines and too afraid to speak them if she had.

Coming quickly to her rescue, Seth opened Rudy's mouth. "I think Tabby's waiting for me to introduce her friend. After all, she is my date, so it's probably the right thing to do." The dummy's head swiveled to the left, and one of his doe eyes winked at Rosie. "This is Rosie Wrong, but someday I hope to right that wrong and make her my bride. Then she'll be Rosie Right, who's always right, because she married me—Rudy Right!"

The audience roared and clapped their approval. Tabby felt herself begin to relax a little, and she was even able to make her dummy say a few words.

"What makes you think I'd marry a dummy?" Rosie announced. "Do I look stupid?"

"No, but you sure are cute!" Rudy shot back.

More laughter from the audience. This was fun—almost. What was Tabby going to do once Seth and Rudy left the stage? So far, she'd only spoken for Rosie. How would things go when she was forced to speak herself?

Rudy and Rosie bantered back and forth a bit longer, then finally Seth said the words Tabby had been dreading. "Well, folks, I think it's time for Rudy and me to say good-bye. I'll leave you in the capable hands of Tabby and her friend, Rosie. I'm sure they have lots of fun up their sleeves." With that, Seth grabbed Rudy and his stand and marched off the stage. The audience clapped, and Tabby nearly panicked. She forgot to pray, and in her own strength, she tried to concentrate on her routine. Everything Seth had told her seemed like ancient history. She couldn't think of anything except trying to please the audience and the paralyzing fear that held her in its grip.

"Say, R–Rosie, h–have you h–heard any good elephant j–jokes lately?" she finally squeaked.

"Oh, sure. Would you like to hear them?" Rosie responded.

Tabby only nodded. One less sentence to stammer through.

"Why do elephants have wrinkles?" Rosie asked.

"I d–don't know."

"Well, for goodness' sake, have you ever tried to iron one?"

A few snickers came from the audience, but it was nothing compared to the belly laughs Seth had gotten. This did little to bolster Tabby's confidence, and she struggled to remember the rest of her performance.

"I sure wish I had enough money to buy an elephant," Rosie said.

"Why w–would you—you w–want an el–elephant?"

"I don't. I just want the money."

Tabby paused, hoping the audience would catch on to the little joke, but they didn't. Not even Donna laughed. Tabby felt like a deflated balloon. So much for the confidence she thought she might have gained. She was failing miserably at entertaining this audience, much less bringing any glory to God through her so-called talent. Then there was Seth. What must he think of his star pupil now? He was probably as mortified as she was, and she couldn't blame him one little bit.

"M–money isn't everything, R–Rosie," Tabby said.

"It's all I need."

"Do y–you know w–what the Bible says about m–money?"

"No, do you?"

Tabby did know what it said, but for the life of her, she couldn't remember. In fact, she had no idea what to say or do next. The audience looked bored with her routine, and she'd done nothing but tell stale jokes and stutter ever since Seth took his leave. Her hands were shaking so badly she could hardly hold Rosie still, and her legs felt like two sticks made of rubber. If she didn't get off this platform soon, she would probably pass out cold.

Tabby drew in a deep breath, grabbed Rosie up in one quick swoop, and darted off the stage.

sixteen

Tabby was sobbing hysterically by the time she reached the room offstage. With all Seth's encouragement, she'd almost begun to believe she did have some talent, but she'd blown it big time. She had let God down, disappointed Seth, and made a complete fool of herself in front of nearly two hundred people! How could she have let this happen? Why hadn't she just told Seth no? All she wanted to do was go home, jump into bed, and bury her head under the covers.

She felt Seth's arms go around her waist. "It's okay, Tabby," he murmured against her ear. "This was your first time, and you were a little nervous, that's all. It's happened to everyone, and it will get easier with time and practice." He slid his hand up to her back and began patting it, as though that would somehow bring her comfort. "You'll do better next time, I'm sure of it."

Tabby pulled away sharply. "There won't be a next time, Seth! Except for the day care kids, I'll never have another audience."

"Yes, you will. You could be perfect if you'd give yourself half a chance. Please, let me help you. . . ."

It seemed as though Seth was asking her to be perfect at ventriloquism, but some of the things she'd heard him say to both Donna and herself made Tabby wonder if what Seth really wanted was for her to be perfect.

"You've helped me enough!" she cried. "Thanks to you, I made myself look like a total idiot out there!"

Before Seth could offer a rebuttal, Tabby jerked the door open. "Find someone else to help," she called over her shoulder.

"I'll never be perfect, and I'm not the woman you need!" Slamming the door, she dashed down the hall. Despite the tears blinding her eyes, Tabby could see someone standing by the front door of the church. It was Donna.

Tabby shook her head. "Don't even say it. I don't want your pity or any kind of sappy pep talk about how things will go better next time."

Donna opened her mouth to say something, but Tabby yanked on the door handle, raced down the steps, and headed straight for her car. All she wanted was to be left alone.

੩ٮ

The next few weeks were filled with mounting tension. Tabby barely spoke to anyone, and Donna kept trying to draw her into a conversation. Seth phoned several times, but Tabby wouldn't accept any of his calls. He even dropped by the day care on two occasions, but she refused to talk to him. It pained her to think she'd fallen in love with a man who couldn't accept her for the way she was. If he wanted "perfect," then he might be better off with someone like Cheryl Stone. Why hadn't he asked her to fill in for the ventriloquist who couldn't do the routine for the crusade? At least Cheryl wouldn't have humiliated herself or Seth in front of a church full of people.

A phone call from her parents, a week later, threw Tabby into deeper depression. On Friday night they would be hosting an engagement party for Lois. Tabby was expected to come, of course. She had always been obligated to attend family functions, even if no one seemed to notice she was there. If she didn't go, she'd probably never hear the end of it, but it irked her that they waited until the last minute to extend an invitation. There was hardly enough time to buy a suitable gift.

The party was set for six-thirty, and it was a good forty-five-minute drive from Tacoma to Olympia. That was barring any unforeseen traffic jams on the freeway. Tabby knew she'd have to leave for Olympia by five-thirty. The day care was open until six-thirty, but Donna said she and their helper could manage alone for an hour.

❧

Seth was fit to be tied. His phone calls to Tabby and his trips to the day care had been for nothing. No matter how much he pleaded, she still refused to talk to him. He could understand her being upset about the routine she'd botched at the crusade. That didn't excuse her for staying mad at him, though.

Sitting at his workbench, mechanically sanding the arm of a new vent figure, Seth sulked. At first he'd only thought of Tabby as someone who needed his help. Then he began to see her as a friend. Finally, he realized he could love her, but she just didn't fit his mold for the "perfect" wife.

Even though they hadn't known each other very long, Seth cared a lot about Tabby and only wanted the best for her. She'd accused him of trying to change her. Maybe it was true. If he were being totally honest, he'd have to admit he did want her to be different—to fit into his special design and become the kind of person he wanted her to be. Tabby might be right. Perhaps he should find someone more suited to him. Maybe Cheryl Stone would be a better match. She had talent, confidence, and beauty. There was just one problem. . . . He wasn't in love with Cheryl. The truth of this revelation slammed into Seth with such force, it left him with a splitting headache. Until this very moment, he'd never really admitted it. He was actually in love with Tabby Johnson, and not for what she could be, but rather for who she was—gentle and sweet spirited with children, humble and never bragging, compassionate and helpful—all the qualities of a true Christian.

Seth left his seat and moved toward the front door of his shop. He put the "closed" sign in the window, then turned off the lights. What he really needed was a long talk with God, followed by a good night's sleep. Maybe he could think things through more clearly in the morning.

ॐ

"Are you sure you don't want me to go with you tonight?" Donna asked Tabby as she prepared to leave the day care center.

Tabby shook her head. "This shindig is for family members only—our side and the groom's. Besides, you've got another date with Alex, remember?"

Donna shrugged. "I know how much you dread being with your family. If I were there, it might buffer things a bit. I could call Alex and cancel."

"Not on your life! It's taken you forever to get past your fear of dating a PK. Don't ruin it by breaking a date when it's totally unnecessary." Tabby waved her hand. "Besides, I'm a grown woman. As you've pointed out many times, it's high time I learn to deal with my family without having someone there to hold my hand."

Donna squeezed Tabby's arm. "Okay, try to have fun tonight, and please, drive carefully."

Tabby wrinkled her nose. "Don't I always?"

"It's not your driving I'm worried about. It's all those maniacs who exceed the speed limit and act as if they own the whole road."

"I'll be careful," Tabby promised as she went out the door.

ॐ

Tabby was glad she'd left in plenty of time, because the freeway was terrible this night. She was tempted to take the next exit and travel the back roads, but the traffic was so congested, she wasn't sure she could even move over a lane in order to get off. By the time she finally pulled off at the Olympia exit, Tabby was a bundle of nerves.

She knew part of her apprehension was because she was about to enter the lions' den. At least, that's the way it always felt whenever she did anything that involved her family. If only Mom and Dad could love and accept her the way they did Lois. If only she was the kind of daughter they wanted. What exactly did they want? Beauty. . .brains. . .boldness? Lois had all three, and she'd been Dad's favorite ever since she was born. But what parent in their right mind would love one child more than another?

Tabby clenched her teeth. Everyone wanted her to change. Was there anyone willing to accept her just the way she was? Donna used to, but lately she'd been pressing Tabby to step out in faith and begin using her talents to serve the Lord. *If I ever have any children of my own, I'll love them all the same, no matter how different they might be.*

Then there was Seth. Tabby thought at first he just wanted to help her, but she was quite sure now he'd been trying to make her over ever since they first met. Was she really so unappealing the way she was? Must she become a whole new person in order for her family and friends to love and accept her?

A verse of Scripture from Second Corinthians popped into her mind: "Therefore, if anyone is in Christ, he is a new creation; the old has gone, the new has come!"

Tabby had accepted the Lord at an early age. She knew she'd been cleansed of her sins, which made her a "new creation." Her stuttering problem and lack of confidence had made her unwilling to completely surrender her life to Christ and let Him use all her talents, though. If she were really a new creation, shouldn't she be praying and asking the Lord's help to become all she could be? She hadn't prayed or kept her focus on Jesus the other night at the church program. Instead, she'd been trying to impress the audience.

"I'll think about this later," Tabby murmured as she turned into her parents' driveway. Her primary concern right now was making it through Lois's engagement party.

Seth was tired of dodging his problems. With Bible in hand and a glass of cold lemonade, he took a seat at the kitchen table, determined to relinquish his own selfish desires and seek God's will for his life.

The first passage of Scripture he came to was in Matthew. Jesus was teaching the Beatitudes to a crowd of people. Seth read verse five aloud. " 'Blessed are the meek, for they will inherit the earth.' "

He propped his elbows on the table and leaned his chin against his palms. "Hmm. . .Tabby fits that category, all right."

He jumped down to verse eight. " 'Blessed are the pure in heart, for they will see God.' " How could he have been so blind? Purity seemed to emanate from Tabby. Morally, she seemed like a clear, crisp mountain stream, untouched by the world's pollution.

Seth turned to the Book of Proverbs, knowing the thirty-first chapter addressed the subject of an honorable wife. " 'A wife of noble character who can find? She is worth far more than rubies.' " He scanned the rest of the chapter, stopping to read verse thirty. " 'Charm is deceptive, and beauty is fleeting; but a woman who fears the LORD is to be praised.' "

Praised. Not ridiculed, coerced, or changed into something other than what she was. Seth placed one hand on the open Bible. He knew he'd found a good thing when he met Tabitha Johnson. Even though she was shy and couldn't always speak without stuttering, she had a generous heart and loved the Lord. Wasn't that what he really wanted in a wife?

Seth bowed his head and closed his eyes. "Dear Lord, forgive me for wanting Tabby to change. You love her just as she is, and I should too. Please give me the chance to make amends. If she's the woman You have in mind for me, then work out the details and make her heart receptive to my love. Amen."

Unexpected tears fell from Seth's eyes, and he sniffed. He

had to talk to Tabby right away, while the truth of God's Word was still fresh on his heart. Praying as he dialed the telephone, Seth petitioned God to give him the right words.

When Donna answered, Seth asked for Tabby.

"She's not home," Donna said. She sounded as though she was either in a hurry or trying to put him off. Was Tabby still too angry to speak with him? Had she asked Donna to continue monitoring her phone calls?

"I really do need to speak with her," Seth said with a catch in his voice. "It's important."

"I'm not giving you the runaround, Seth. Tabby isn't home right now."

"Where is she?"

"She left work a little early and drove to Olympia."

"Why'd she go there?"

"It's where her parents live. They're having an engagement party for her sister, Lois."

"Oh." Seth blew out his breath. If Tabby was in Olympia, she probably wouldn't get home until late. There would be no chance of talking to her until tomorrow.

"I'd like to talk more, Seth, but my date just arrived," Donna said.

He groaned. "Yeah, okay. Tell Tabby I'll call her tomorrow." Seth hung up the phone and leaned his head on the table. Why was it that whenever he made a decision to do something, there always seemed to be some kind of roadblock? If only he'd committed this situation to God a bit sooner.

"Guess all I can do is put things in Your hands, Lord. . . which is exactly where they should have been in the first place."

seventeen

Tabby's mother greeted her at the door with a frown. "You're late. Everyone else is here already."

Tabby glanced at her watch. It was ten minutes to seven. She was only twenty minutes late. She chose not to make an issue of it, though, merely shrugging and handing her mother the small bag she was holding. "Here's my g–gift for L–Lois."

Mom took the gift and placed it on a table just inside the living room door. "Come in. Everyone's in the backyard, waiting for your father to finish barbecuing the sirloin steaks."

Tabby grimaced. Apparently Dad was going all out for his favorite daughter. *If I were engaged, I doubt I'd even be given an engagement party, much less one with all the trimmings. And even if there were a party in my honor, Dad would probably fix plain old hamburgers, instead of a select, choice cut of meat.*

"How was the freeway tonight?" Mom asked as she and Tabby made their way down the hallway, leading to the back of their modest but comfortable, split-level home.

"Bad. R–really bad. That's w–why I'm l–late," Tabby mumbled.

Mom didn't seem to be listening. She was scurrying about the kitchen, looking through every drawer and cupboard as if her life depended upon finding whatever it was she was searching for.

"C–can I help w–with anything?" Tabby asked.

"I suppose you can get the jug of iced tea from the refrigerator. I've got to find the long-handled fork for your father. He sent me in here five minutes ago to look for it."

Tabby crossed the room, opened the refrigerator, grabbed the iced tea, and started for the back door.

"Wait a minute," Mom called. "I found the fork. Would you take it out to Dad?"

"Aren't you c—coming?" Tabby took the fork from her mother and waited expectantly.

"I'll be out in a minute. I just need to check on my pan of baked beans."

Tabby shrugged and headed out the door, wishing she could be anywhere else but here.

About twenty people were milling around the Johnsons' backyard. Some she recognized as aunts, uncles, and cousins. Then there was Grandma Haskins, Dad, Lois, and her sister's wealthy fiancé, Michael Yehley. Some faces were new to her. She assumed those were people related to the groom.

"I see you finally decided to join us," Dad said gruffly, when Tabby handed him the barbecue fork. "Ever since you were a kid, you've been slow. Yep, slower than a turtle plowing through peanut butter. How come you're always late for everything?"

Peanut butter, Tabby mused. *That's what Seth has a fear of eating.* It seemed that lately everything made her think about Seth. She wouldn't even allow Dad's little put-down to rattle her as much as usual. She was too much in love. There, she'd finally admitted it—at least to herself. *For all the good it will do me. Seth doesn't have a clue how I feel, and even if he did, it wouldn't matter. He sees me only as a friend—someone to help out of her shell.* She frowned. *Besides, I'm still mad at him for coercing me into doing that dumb vent routine.*

"Are you just going to stand there like a dummy, or is there some justification for you being so late?" Dad bellowed, snapping Tabby out of her musings.

"I w—wasn't l—l—late on pur—pur—purpose," she stammered. She always stuttered worse around Dad. Maybe it was because he was the one person she wanted most to please. "Tr–traffic was r–really h–h–heavy."

"Why didn't you take off work early so you could get here on time?" Dad said, jerking the fork out of Tabby's hand.

She winced. "I—I d–did l–leave early." Tears hung on her lashes, but she refused to cry.

Dad turned back to the barbecue grill without saying anything more. Tabby pirouetted toward her grandmother, knowing she would at least have a kind word or two.

Grandma Haskins, cheerfully dressed in a long floral skirt and a pink ruffled blouse, greeted Tabby with a peck on the cheek. "It's good to see you, Dear." She tipped her silver-gray head to one side. "You're looking kind of peaked. Are you eating right and getting plenty of sleep? You're not coming down with anything, I hope."

Tabby couldn't help but smile. Grandma was always worrying about something. Since she saw Tabby so seldom, it was only fitting that she'd be her target tonight. Tabby didn't really mind, though. It felt kind of nice to have someone fussing over her. Ever since she'd made a fool of herself at the crusade, she had been wallowing in self-pity. Maybe a few minutes with Grandma would make her feel better. "I'm f–fine, Grandma, r–really," she mumbled.

Tabby and Grandma were about to find a place to sit down, when Lois came rushing up. Her face was flushed, and she looked as though she might have been crying.

"What's wrong, Lois?" Grandma asked in a tone of obvious concern.

Lois sniffed deeply and motioned them toward one of the empty tables. As soon as they sat down, she began to cry.

Tabby gave her sister's arm a gentle squeeze. "C–can you t–tell us about it?"

Lois hiccupped loudly and wiped at her eyes, which only smudged her black mascara, making the tears look like little drops of mud rolling down her cheeks. "It's Mike!" she wailed.

"Is something wrong with Michael?" Grandma asked. "I saw him a little while ago, and he looked fine to me."

"Oh, he's fine all right," Lois ranted. "He's so fine that he's decided to take over the planning of our wedding."

"Isn't that the b–bride's job?" Tabby inquired.

"I thought so, until this evening." Lois blew her nose on a napkin and scowled. She didn't look nearly as beautiful tonight as she had the last time Tabby had seen her. That was the night of Tabby's birthday party. Lois didn't have little rivulets of coal-colored tears streaming down her face then.

"Tell us what happened," Grandma prompted.

Lois looked around the yard anxiously. Her gaze came to rest on her fiancé, sitting with some of his family at another table.

Tabby glanced that way as well. She was surprised when Mike looked over and scowled. At least she thought it was a scowl. Maybe he'd just eaten one of Mom's famous stuffed mushrooms. Tabby didn't know why, but those mushrooms always tasted like they'd been filled with toothpaste instead of cream cheese.

"Mike doesn't want us to get married the first Saturday in October after all," Lois whined, jerking Tabby's thoughts back to the situation at hand.

"He doesn't?" Grandma handed Lois another napkin. "Does he want to call the whole thing off?"

Lois drew in a shuddering breath. "He says not, but I have to wonder. Mike thinks we should have more time to get to know one another before we tie the knot. He wants to postpone the wedding until June, and he waited 'til tonight to drop the bomb."

"June?" Grandma exclaimed. "Why, that's ten months away!"

"That's not a b–bad idea," Tabby interjected. "I mean,

s–sometimes you th–think you know a p–person, and then he g–goes and does something to r–really throw you a c–curve ball."

Grandma and Lois both turned their attention on Tabby. "Are you talking about anyone in particular?" Grandma asked.

Tabby shook her head. "No, n–not r–really." She had no intention of telling them about Seth. They'd never understand the way things were. Besides, they weren't supposed to be talking about her right now. This was Lois's engagement party, and apparently there wasn't going to be a wedding. . . at least not this year. "Do M–Mom and D–Dad know yet?" she asked.

Lois shook her head. "I only found out myself a few minutes ago." She reached for Tabby's hand and gripped it tightly. "What am I going to do?"

Tabby swallowed hard. She could hardly believe that her confident, all-knowing little sister was asking her advice. If only she had the right answers. Thinking back to the devotions she'd done that morning, Tabby quoted the following Scripture: " 'Do not let your heart be troubled. Trust in God, trust also in me.' "

Lois's face was pinched, and her eyes were mere slits. "What on earth are you talking about? Why would I trust in you? What can you do to help my situation?"

Tabby bit back the laughter rising in her throat. Even though she and Lois had both gone to Sunday school when they were children, Lois had never shown much interest in the things of God. In fact, she'd quit going to church when she turned thirteen. "That verse from the Book of John is saying you should trust God and not allow your troubles to overtake you. 'Trust in God; trust also in Me.' That was Jesus speaking, and He was telling His followers to trust in Him, as well as in God." Tabby smiled at her sister. "As I'm sure you already know, Jesus and God are one and the same. So, if you put your trust in God, you're trusting Jesus too."

Lois's mouth was hanging wide open, and Grandma was looking at Tabby as though she'd never seen her before.

"What? What's wrong?" Tabby questioned.

"Do you realize you just quoted that Bible verse and gave me a little pep talk without missing a single word? No stuttering, no stammering, nothing," Lois announced. "I think that must be a first, don't you, Grandma?"

Grandma smiled. "I wouldn't say it was a first, because I can remember when Tabby was a little girl and didn't have a problem with stuttering." She reached over and gave Tabby's hand a gentle pat. "I think it's safe to say when Tabby feels convicted about something, she forgets her insecurities, so her words flow uninterrupted."

Tabby wasn't sure how to respond to Grandma's comment, but she never had a chance to, because Lois cut right in. "Well, be that as it may, it doesn't solve my problem with Mike. How am I going to convince him to marry me in two months? I'll just die if I have to wait until next summer."

Grandma's hand made an arc as it left Tabby's and landed on Lois's. "Everything will work out, Dear. Just do as Tabby says, and put your trust in the Lord."

Tabby looked over at her grandmother, and her heart swelled with love. If Grandma was beginning to believe, maybe there was some hope for the rest of the family. With more prayer and reliance on God, there might even be some hope for her. Perhaps she just needed to trust the Lord a bit more.

eighteen

When rain started falling around eight o'clock, everyone went inside. Tabby decided to head for home, knowing the roads would probably be bad. Besides, she was anxious to be by herself. This had been some evening. First, her parents' little put-downs, then the news that Lois wasn't getting married in October, followed by that special time she, Grandma, and Lois had shared. For a few brief moments, Tabby had felt lifted out of her problems and experienced a sense of joy by offering support to her sister. If only Lois hadn't ended up throwing a temper tantrum right before the party ended. She and Mike had spent most of the evening arguing, and when they weren't quarreling, Lois was crying. Tabby couldn't help but feel sorry for her.

"No matter when the wedding is, you can keep the automatic two-cup coffeemaker I gave you tonight," Tabby told Lois just before she left. She said good-bye to the rest of the family and climbed into her car. It had been a long week, and she'd be so glad to get home and into bed. Maybe some reading in the Psalms would help too. Despite his troubles, David had a way of searching his soul and looking to God for all the answers to his problems and frustrations. Tabby needed that daily reminder as well.

&

The freeway was still crowded, though it was not quite as bad as it had been earlier. To make matters worse, the rain was coming down so hard Tabby could barely see out her windshield. She gripped the steering wheel with determination and prayed for all she was worth.

146

By the time Tabby reached the Lakewood exit, she'd had enough. She turned on her right blinker and signaled to get off. Traveling the back roads through Lakewood, Fircrest, then into Tacoma would be easier than trying to navigate the freeway traffic and torrential rains. At least she could travel at a more leisurely pace, and she'd be able to pull off the road if necessary.

Tabby clicked on her car radio as she headed down the old highway. The local Christian station was playing a song by a new female artist. The words played over and over in Tabby's head. *Jesus is your strength, give to Him your all. . . . Jesus wants your talents, please listen to His call. . . .*

The lyrical tune soothed Tabby's soul and made her think about Seth again. For weeks he'd been telling her to use her talents for the Lord. "That's because he's trying to change me," she murmured. "Seth's more concerned about finding the perfect woman than he is about me using my talents for God."

Even as she said the words, Tabby wondered if they were true. Maybe Seth really did care about her. It could be that he only wanted her to succeed as a ventriloquist so she could serve the Lord better.

"But I am serving the Lord," Tabby moaned. "I bake cookies for shut-ins, take my turn in the church nursery, teach the day care kids about Jesus, tithe regularly, and pray for the missionaries. Shouldn't that be enough?"

As Tabby mulled all this over, she noticed the car in front of her begin to swerve. Was the driver of the small white vehicle drunk, or was it merely the slick road causing the problem? Maybe the man or woman is driving too fast for these hazardous conditions, she reasoned. Tabby eased up on the gas pedal, keeping a safe distance from the car ahead. If the driver decided to slam on his brakes unexpectedly, she wanted plenty of room to stop.

She was on a long stretch of road now, with no houses or

places of business nearby. Only giant fir trees and bushy shrubs dotted the edge of the highway. The vehicle ahead was still swerving, and just as it rounded the next corner, the unthinkable happened. The little car lurched, spun around twice, then headed straight for an embankment. Tabby let out a piercing scream as she watched it disappear over the hill.

Tapping her brakes lightly, so they wouldn't lock, Tabby pulled to the side of the road. Her heart was thumping so hard she thought it might burst, and her palms were so sweaty she could barely open the car door. Stepping out into the rain, Tabby prayed, "Oh, Lord, please let the passengers in that car be okay."

Tabby stood on the edge of the muddy embankment, gazing at the gully below. She could see the white car, flipped upside down. She glanced up at the sky. Tree branches swayed overhead in a crazy green blur, mixed with pelting raindrops. She took a guarded step forward; then with no thought for her own safety, she scrambled down the hill, slipping and sliding with each step. Unmindful of the navy blue flats she wore on her feet or the fact that her long denim skirt was getting splattered with mud, she inched her way toward the overturned vehicle.

When she reached the site of the accident, Tabby noticed the wheels of the car were still spinning, and one tire had the rubber ripped away. Apparently there had been a blowout, which would account for the car's sudden swerving.

Tabby dashed to the driver's side. The window was broken, and she could see a young woman with short brown hair, lying on her stomach across the upside-down steering wheel. There was only a few inches between her head and the roof of the car. She could see from the rise and fall of the woman's back that she was breathing, but her eyes were closed, and she didn't respond when Tabby called out to her.

A pathetic whine drew Tabby's attention to the backseat.

A young child, also on her stomach, called, "Mommy. . . Mommy, help me!"

Tabby's brain felt fuzzy, and her legs were weak and rubbery. She had no idea how to help the woman or her child. She certainly wouldn't be able to get them out by herself, and even if she could, she knew from the recent CPR training she'd taken, it wasn't a good idea to move an accident victim who might have serious injuries. What this woman and child needed was professional help. She'd have to go back to the car and call 911 on her cell phone. If only she'd thought to grab it before she made her spontaneous descent.

"D–don't be afraid, little g–girl," Tabby called to the child. "I'm g–going to my c–car and c–call for help. I'll b–be right b–back."

The blond-haired girl, who appeared to be about five years old, began to sob. "I don't know you, and you talk funny. Go away!"

A feeling of frustration, mixed with icy fingers of fear, held Tabby in its grip. She hated to leave but knew she had to. "I'll b–be right b–back," she promised.

As she scrambled up the hill, Tabby could still hear the child's panicked screams. They tore at her heart and made her move as quickly as possible. By the time she reached her car, Tabby was panting, and her fears were mounting. What if the car was leaking gas? What if it caught on fire and she couldn't get the passengers out in time? The stark terror that had inched its way into her head, was now fully in control. She felt paralyzed of both body and mind.

She offered up another quick prayer and slid into the car, then reached into the glove box for her cell phone. With trembling fingers, she dialed 911. When an operator came on, Tabby stuttered and stammered so badly the woman had to ask her to repeat the information several times. Tabby was finally assured that help was on the way and was instructed to go back to the car and try to keep the occupants calm.

How in the world am I going to do that? she wondered. *The little girl didn't even want to talk to me.*

Suddenly, Tabby remembered Rosie, who was in the backseat. She'd taken the dummy to work that day, in order to put on a short routine for the day care kids. *Maybe the child will feel less threatened talking to Rosie than she would me.*

Tabby reached over the seat and grabbed the dummy. "Well, Rosie, you're really gonna be put to the test this time."

Back down the hill she went, feeling the squish of mud as it seeped inside her soft leather shoes and worked its way down to her toes. Her clothes were drenched, and her soggy hair hung limply on her shoulders. In the process of her descent, Tabby fell twice. The second time, Rosie flipped out of her arms and landed with a thud on an uprooted tree. Tabby picked her up, only to discover that Rosie's face was dirty and scratched, her head had come loose, and the control stick was jammed. Not only would Rosie's slot-jaw mouth no longer move, but the poor dummy looked a mess!

"Now what am I going to do?" Tabby lamented. "Rosie was my only hope of reaching that child."

"I can do everything through him who gives me strength." The Scripture verse that popped into Tabby's mind offered some comfort and hope. She closed her eyes briefly and pictured the Lord gathering her into His strong arms. He loved her. He cared about her, as well as the two accident victims in that car down there. With His help, Tabby would step boldly out of her shell and serve Him in whatever way He showed her. She could do all things, because of His strength.

"Lord, I really do need Your strength right now. Please calm my heart and let me speak without stuttering, so I can help the little girl not be so afraid."

When Tabby hurried to the car, the child was still crying. She knelt next to the open window and turned Rosie upside down, hoping the sight of the small dummy might make the girl feel better. "This is my friend, Rosie. She wants to be your friend too," Tabby said softly. "Can you tell me your name, Sweetie?"

The child turned her head slightly, and her lips parted in a faint smile. "It's Katie, and I'm almost six."

Tabby released the breath she'd been holding. Progress. They were making a little bit of progress. "Rosie's been hurt, so she can't talk right now," she said. "Why don't the two of us talk, though? Rosie can just listen."

Katie squinted her blue eyes, but finally nodded. "Okay."

Tabby's confidence was being handed over to her. She could feel it. She hadn't expected such a dramatic answer to her prayer, but the doors of timidity were finally swinging open. *Thank You, Lord.* Tabby tipped her head to one side and leaned closer to the window. Now Rosie's head was poking partway in. "Are you hurting anywhere?" she asked Katie.

"My arm's bleedin', and my head kinda hurts," the child said, her blue eyes filling with fresh tears.

"I used my cell phone to call for help," Tabby explained. "The paramedics should be here soon. Then they'll help you and your mommy get out of the car."

Katie choked on a sob. "Mommy won't wake up. I keep callin' her, but she don't answer."

Tabby wasn't sure how to respond. Even though Katie's mom was breathing, she could still be seriously hurt. She might even die. Katie had good reason to be scared.

"Listen, Honey," she said with assurance, "I've been praying for you and your mommy. The Lord is here with us, and help is on the way. Let's talk about other things for now, okay?"

Katie nodded, but tears kept streaming down her bruised cheeks. It tore at Tabby's heartstrings, but she was thankful the child was willing to talk to her now. She was also grateful for answered prayer. Since she'd returned to the battered car, she hadn't stuttered even once.

"What's your last name, Katie?"

There was a long pause, then finally Katie smiled and said, "It's Duncan. My name's Katie Duncan."

"What's your mommy's name?"

"Mommy."

In spite of the stressful circumstances, Tabby had to bite back the laughter bubbling in her throat. Children were so precious. That's why she loved working with the kids at the day care. She'd probably never marry and have children of her own, and being around those little ones helped fill a void in her heart.

"I have a dolly, too, but she's not half as big as yours," Katie said, looking at Rosie.

Tabby chuckled. "Rosie's a ventriloquist dummy. Do you know what that means?"

Katie shook her head.

"She's kind of like a big puppet. I make her talk by pulling a lever inside her body."

"Can you make her talk right now?"

Tabby sucked in her bottom lip. "Rosie's control stick broke when she fell down the hill."

Katie's chin began to quiver, as a fresh set of tears started to seep from her eyes.

"I suppose I could make her talk," Tabby said quickly. "Her mouth won't move, though. Could you pretend Rosie's mouth is moving?"

"Uh-huh. I like to pretend. Mommy and I do pretend tea parties."

"That's good. I like to play make-believe too." Tabby tipped Rosie's head, so Katie could see her better. Using her childlike ventriloquist voice, she said, "I'm Rosie Right, and I'm always right." *Now what made me say that? That's the line Seth always uses with his dummy, Rudy.*

"Nobody but God is always right. Mommy said so," Katie remarked.

Tabby nodded. "Your mommy's right. Rosie's just a puppet. She can't always be right, and neither can people. Only God has all the answers."

"Do you go to school, Rosie?" Katie asked the dummy.

"Sometimes I go to day care," Rosie answered. "Tabby works there."

The next few minutes were spent in friendly banter between Rosie, Tabby, and Katie. Tabby was glad she could keep the child's mind off the accident and her unconscious mother in the front seat, but when a low moan escaped the woman's lips, Tabby froze. Now she had two people to try and keep calm.

nineteen

"Oh! Oh! I can't breathe," Katie's mother moaned. "My seat belt. . .it's too tight."

Tabby pulled Rosie quickly away from the window and placed one hand on the woman's outstretched arm. "Please, try to remain calm."

The woman moaned again. "Who are you?"

"I'm Tabitha Johnson. I was in the car behind you, and I saw your car swerve, then run off the road. You ended up going over the embankment, and now the car's upside down."

"My name is Rachel Duncan, and I need to get this seat belt off. Do you have a knife?"

Tabby shook her head. "That's not a good idea. If we cut the belt loose, your head will hit the roof, and that might cause serious damage if there's a neck injury."

Rachel's eyelids closed, and she groaned. "Katie. . . Where's Katie?"

"Your little girl is still in the backseat," Tabby answered. "We've been visiting while we wait for the paramedics."

"Mommy, Mommy, I'm here!" Katie called.

Rachel's eyes shot open. "I'm so sorry about this, Katie. Mommy doesn't know what happened."

"From the looks of your right front tire, I'd say you had a blowout," Tabby said.

Rachel's swollen lips emitted a shuddering sob. "I told Rick we needed to buy a new set of tires."

"Rick?"

"Rick's my husband. He had to work late tonight, so Katie and I went to a movie in Lakewood. We were on our way home when it started raining really hard." She grimaced. "I hope someone gets us out of here real soon. I don't think I can stand being in this position much longer."

"Are you in pain?" Tabby asked with concern.

"My left leg feels like it might be broken, and my head's pounding something awful."

"Would you mind if I prayed for you?" Tabby didn't know where she'd gotten the courage to ask that question. It wasn't like her to be so bold.

"I'd really appreciate the prayer," Rachel answered. Tears were coursing down her cheeks, but she offered Tabby a weak smile. "I'm a Christian, I know how much prayer can help."

Tabby placed Rosie on the ground and leaned in as far as she could. "Heavenly Father," she prayed, "Rachel and Katie are in pain and need medical attention as soon as possible. I'm asking You to bring the paramedics here quickly. Please give them both a sense of peace and awareness that You are right here beside them."

Tabby had just said "amen" when she heard the piercing whine of sirens in the distance. "That must be the rescue vehicles," she told Rachel. "I think I should go back up the hill to be sure they know where we are. Will you be all right for a few minutes?"

"Jesus is with us," Katie squeaked.

"Yes, He's by our side," Rachel agreed.

"All right then, I'll be back as quick as I can." Tabby pulled away from the window and started up the hill as fast as she could, thankful the rain had finally eased up.

A police car, a fire truck, and the paramedics' rig were pulling off the road by her car when she came over the hill. Gasping for breath, she dashed over to one of the firemen. "There's a car down there," she panted, pointing to the ravine. "It's upside down, and there's a woman and a little girl trapped inside."

"Could you tell if they were seriously injured?" one of the paramedics asked as he stepped up beside her.

"Rachel—she's the mother—said her head hurt real bad, and she thinks her leg might be broken. Katie's only five, and she complained of her head hurting too. She also said her arm was bleeding."

He nodded, then turned to his partner. "Let's grab our gear and get down there."

The rescue squad descended the hill much faster than Tabby had, but she figured they'd had a good deal more practice doing this kind of thing.

Tabby followed, keeping a safe distance once they were at the scene of the accident. She did move in to grab Rosie when a fireman stepped on one of the dummy's hands. Poor, dirty Rosie had enough injuries to keep her in Seth's shop for at least a month. Right now, Tabby's concerns were for Rachel and her precious daughter, though. She kept watching and praying as the rescuers struggled to free the trapped victims.

When they finally had Rachel and Katie loaded into the ambulance, Tabby breathed a sigh of relief. The paramedics said it didn't appear as though either of them had any life-threatening injuries, although there would be tests done at the hospital. Before the ambulance pulled away, Tabby promised Rachel she would call her husband and let him know what happened.

One of the policemen, who identified himself as Officer Jensen, asked Tabby a series of questions about the accident, since she'd been the only witness.

"You are one special young lady," the officer said. "Not only did you call for help, but you stayed to comfort that woman and her daughter." He glanced down at the bedraggled dummy Tabby was holding. "From the looks of your little friend, I'd say you went the extra mile, using your talent in a time of need."

Tabby smiled, although she felt like crying. For the first time in a long while, she'd forgotten her fears and self-consciousness, allowing God to speak through her in a way she never thought possible. Throughout the entire ordeal, she'd never stuttered once. It seemed like a miracle—one she hoped would last forever. Up until now, she believed that unless her family treated her with love and respect, she could never become confident. How wrong she'd been. How grateful to God she felt now.

When Tabby got into her car, she reached for the cell phone and called Rick Duncan at the number Rachel had given her. He was shocked to hear about the accident but thankful Tabby had called. He told her he'd leave work right away and head straight for Tacoma General Hospital. Tabby could finally go home, knowing Rachel, Katie, and Rick were in God's hands.

≈

Tabby awoke the following morning feeling as though she'd run a ten-mile marathon and hadn't been in shape for it. The emotional impact of the night before hit her hard. If she could get through something so frightening, she was sure the Lord would see her through anything—even dealing with her unfeeling parents and self-centered sister. Instead of shying away from family gatherings or letting someone's harsh words cut her to the quick, Tabby's plan was to stand behind the Lord's shield of protection. She could do all things through Him, and as soon as she had some breakfast, she planned to phone Tacoma General Hospital and check on Rachel's and Katie's conditions. Then her next order of business would be to visit Beyers' Ventriloquist Studio.

≈

Seth had dialed Tabby's phone number four times in the last fifteen minutes, and it was always busy. "Who is on the phone, and who could she be talking to?" he muttered.

"Maybe I should get in my car and drive on over there."

Seth figured Tabby was still mad at him, and he wondered if she'd even let him into her apartment. Well, he didn't care if she was mad. He'd made up his mind to see her today.

Seth left the red-nosed clown dummy he'd been working on and walked into the main part of his shop just as the bell on the front door jingled. In walked Cheryl Stone.

"Good morning, Seth," she purred. "How are you today?"

Seth's heart sank. The blue-eyed woman staring up at him with a hopeful smile was not the person he most wanted to see. "Hi, Cheryl. What brings you here this morning?"

"Does there have to be a reason?" Cheryl tipped her head to one side and offered him another coquettish smile.

Seth felt the force of her softly spoken words like a blow to the stomach. Cheryl was obviously interested in him. "Most people don't come to my shop without a good reason," he mumbled. "Are you having a problem with Oscar again?"

Cheryl gave the ends of her long red hair a little flick and moved slowly toward Seth. "Actually, I'm not here about either one of my dummies."

Seth swallowed hard and took a few steps back. *Now here's a perfect woman. She's talented, confident, poised, and beautiful. How come I don't go after her?* He groaned inwardly. *I'm in love with Tabby Johnson, that's why.* There was no denying it, either. Shy, stuttering Tabitha, with eyes that reminded him of a wounded deer, had stolen his heart, and he'd been powerless to stop it.

With determination, Seth pulled his thoughts away from Tabby and onto the matter at hand. "Why are you here, Cheryl?"

"I've been asked to be part of a talent contest sponsored by Valley Foods. My father works in the corporate office there," Cheryl explained.

"What's that got to do with me?"

"I was hoping you'd be willing to give me a few extra lessons." She giggled. "I know I'm already a good ventriloquist, but I think you're about the best around. Some more helpful tips from you might help me win that contest."

Seth cleared his throat, hoping to stall for time. At least long enough so he could come up with some legitimate excuse for not helping Cheryl. He had an inkling she had a bit more in mind than just ventriloquist lessons.

His suspicions were confirmed when she stepped forward and threw her arms around his neck. The smell of apricot shampoo filled his nostrils, as a wisp of her soft red hair brushed against his cheek.

"Please say you'll do this for me, Seth," Cheryl pleaded as she placed her arms around his neck. "Pretty please. . .with sugar and spice. . .now don't make me ask twice."

Seth moaned. Cheryl was mere inches from his face now, but all he could think about was Tabby. He opened his mouth to give Cheryl his answer, when the bell on the door jingled. Over the top of Cheryl's head, he saw the door swing wide open.

It was Tabitha Johnson.

twenty

Seth expected Tabby to turn around and run out the door once she saw Cheryl in his arms. She didn't, though. Instead, she marched up to the counter and plunked her dummy down. "I'm sorry to interrupt," she said in a voice filled with surprising confidence, "but I need you to take a look at Rosie. Do you think you can spare a few minutes, Seth?"

Seth reached up to pull Cheryl's arms away from his neck. He was guilty of nothing, yet he felt like a kid who'd been caught with his hand inside a candy dish. He could only imagine what Tabby must be thinking, walking in and seeing what looked like a romantic interlude between him and Cheryl.

He studied Tabby for a few seconds. She looked different today—cute and kind of spunky. Her hair was curled, too, and it didn't hang in her face the way it usually did. Her blue jeans and yellow T-shirt were neatly pressed, and she stood straighter than normal.

"Do you have time to look at Rosie or not?" Tabby asked again.

Seth nodded, feeling as if he were in a daze. Tabby wasn't even stuttering. What happened to Timid Tabitha with the doe eyes? He glanced down at Cheryl and noticed she was frowning. "Excuse me, but I have to take care of business," he said, hoping she'd get the hint and leave.

Cheryl planted both hands on her slim hips and whirled around to face Tabby. "Can't you see that Seth and I are busy?"

"I'll only keep Seth a few minutes; then he's all yours," Tabby said through tight lips.

A muscle in Seth's jaw twitched. "I'll call you later, Cheryl," he said, turning toward the counter where the dummy lay.

"Yeah, okay," Cheryl mumbled.

When he heard the door close, Seth heaved a sigh of relief. At least one problem had been resolved.

&

Tabby was trembling inwardly, but outwardly she was holding up quite well—thanks to the Lord and the prayer she'd uttered when she first walked into Seth's shop. Seeing Cheryl Stone in Seth's arms had nearly been her undoing. Only God's grace kept her from retreating into her old shell and allowing her tongue to run wild with a bunch of stuttering and stammering. It still amazed her that ever since the car accident last night she hadn't stuttered once. God really had changed her life.

"What in the world happened to Rosie?" Seth asked, breaking into Tabby's thoughts. "She looks like she got roped into a game of mud wrestling. I'd say she came out on the losing end of things."

Tabby snickered. "It was something like that." Then, feeling the need to talk about what happened last night, she opened up and shared the entire story of the accident she'd witnessed.

Seth listened intently as he examined the dummy. When Tabby finished talking, he looked up from his work and groaned softly. "I'm sure thankful you're okay. You were smart to keep a safe distance from that car when it began to swerve. It could have been your little hatchback rolling down the hill."

Tabby swallowed hard. Was Seth really concerned about her welfare? Was that frown he wore proof of his anxiety?

"Now about Rosie. . . ," Seth said, pulling her back to the immediate need.

"How bad is the damage? Will Rosie ever talk again?"

Seth's green eyes met Tabby's with a gaze that bore straight into her soul. "She will if you want her to."

Tabby blinked. "Of course, I do. Why wouldn't I?"

Seth cleared his throat a few times, as though searching for the right words. "After that program at the crusade, you didn't seem any too anxious to continue using your ventriloquistic talents."

She nodded. "You're right about that, but since last night I'm seeing things in a whole new light."

He raised his eyebrows. "You are? In what way?"

"For one thing, God showed me that I don't have to be afraid of people or circumstances which might seem a bit unusual or disturbing," she explained. "I was really scared when that car went over the embankment. When I found Rachel and her daughter trapped inside their overturned vehicle, I nearly panicked." Tabby drew in a deep breath and squeezed her lips together. "Little Katie wouldn't even respond to me at first. I was stuttering so much I scared her. Then I thought about Rosie in the backseat of my car, and I climbed back up the hill to get her."

Seth nodded. "Kids will react to a dummy much quicker than they will an adult." He smiled. "Guess we're a bit too intimidating."

"I dropped Rosie on the way down the hill, and by the time I got to the wreck, I realized her mouth control was broken." Tabby shrugged. "I had to talk on my own, and I asked God to help me do it without stuttering. I wanted Katie to be able to understand every word, so she wouldn't be afraid."

"So poor Rosie took a trip down the muddy incline for nothing?" Seth asked, giving the dummy's head a few taps with his knuckle.

Tabby shook her head. "Not really. After Katie and I talked awhile, I began to gain her confidence. Then I put Rosie up to the window and made her talk, without even moving her lips."

Seth tipped his head back and roared.

"What's so funny?"

"If Rosie's lips weren't moving, then who was the ventriloquist, and who was the dummy?"

Tabby giggled and reached out to poke Seth playfully in the ribs. "Ha! Very funny!" She wiggled her nose. "I'll have you know, Mr. Beyers, my dummy is so talented, she can talk for two without moving her lips!"

Seth grinned, and his eyes sparkled mischievously. "And you, Miss Tabitha Johnson, are speaking quite well on your own today."

Tabby felt herself blush. "I haven't stuttered once since last night." She placed her palms against her burning cheeks. "God gave me confidence I never thought I would have, and I'm so grateful."

"I think it was because you finally put yourself fully in His hands."

Tabby was tempted to ask Seth if he thought she was worthy of his love now. After all, he'd wanted her to change. Instead of voicing her thoughts, she nodded toward Rosie. "Is there any hope for her?"

Seth scratched the back of his head and smiled. "I think with a little help from some of my tools and a new coat of paint, Rosie will be up and around in no time at all."

Tabby smiled gratefully, but then she sobered. "Will the repairs be expensive?"

Seth winked, and she pressed a hand to a heart that was beating much too fast.

"Let's see now. . . The price for parts will be reimbursed with two or three dinners out, and labor. . .well, I'm sure we can work something out for that as well," Seth said, never taking his gaze off her. "Something that will be agreeable to both of us." He moved slowly toward her, with both arms extended.

Tabby had an overwhelming desire to rush into those strong arms and declare her undying love, but she held herself in check, remembering the little scene she'd encountered when she first entered Seth's shop. It was obvious that Seth had more than a business relationship with Cheryl.

Seth kept moving closer, until she could feel his warm breath on her upturned face. She trembled, and her eyelids drifted shut. Tabby knew she shouldn't let Seth kiss her—not when he was seeing someone else. Her heart said something entirely different, though, and it was with her whole heart that Tabby offered her lips willingly to Seth's inviting kiss.

Tabby relished in the warmth of Seth's embrace, until the sharp ringing of the telephone pulled them apart.

"Uh, guess I'd better get that," Seth mumbled. He stepped away from Tabby and moved across the room toward the desk where the phone sat.

Tabby looked down at Rosie and muttered, "I think I was just saved by the bell."

ða

As Seth answered the phone, his thoughts were focused on Tabby. He'd wanted to hold her longer and tell her everything that was tumbling around in his mind. He needed to express his feelings about the way he'd treated her in the past and share the Scriptures the Lord had shown him. Maybe they'd be able to pick up where they left off when he hung up the phone. Maybe. . .

"Seth Beyers," he said numbly into the receiver. "Huh? Oh, yeah, I'd be happy to take a look at your dummy. I'm about to close shop for the day, but you can bring it by on Monday."

Relieved to be off the phone, Seth returned to Tabby. She was standing over Rosie, looking as though she'd lost her best friend. "She'll be okay, I promise," he said, reaching out to pull Tabby into his arms. He leaned over and placed a kiss on her forehead. Her hair felt feathery soft against his lips, and it smelled like sunshine.

She pulled sharply away, taking him by surprise. She'd seemed willing a few minutes ago. What had happened in the space of a few minutes to make her so cold?

"How long 'til she's done?" Tabby asked.

"I could probably get her ready to go home in about a week. How's that sound?"

She shrugged. "That'll be fine, I guess." She turned and started for the door.

"Hey, where are you going?" he called after her.

"Home. I left the apartment before Donna got up, and since I came home so late last night, I promised to fill her in on the accident details this morning."

Seth rushed to her side. "Don't tell me I'll be taking the day off for nothing."

She blinked several times. "I don't get it. What's your taking the day off got to do with me?"

"I'd really like to spend the day with you. That is, if you're not tied up."

"I just told you. . ."

"I know. You want to tell Donna about last night." Seth grabbed Tabby's arm and pulled her to his side again. "Can't that wait awhile? We have some important things to discuss, and I thought we could do it at the park."

"Point Defiance?"

He nodded.

Tabby hung her head. He knew she was weakening, because she'd told him before how much she loved going to Point Defiance Park.

"Wouldn't that be kind of like a date?" she murmured.

He laughed. "Not kind of, Tabby. . .it is a date."

"Oh. Well, I guess my answer has to be no."

His forehead creased. "Why, for goodness' sake? Are you still mad at me for coercing into doing that vent routine?"

She shook her head. "No, I've done what the Bible says and forgiven you. Besides, what happened at the crusade was really my own fault. I could have said no when you asked me to perform. I could have prayed more and allowed God to speak through me, instead of letting myself get all tied up in knots, and ending up making my routine and me look completely ridiculous."

Seth gently touched her arm. "Neither you nor your routine was ridiculous, Tabby." He chewed on his lower lip, praying silently for the right words to express his true feelings. "Tabby, you're not the only one God's been working on lately."

"What do you mean?"

"Through the Scriptures, He's showed me that I've been expecting too much. I wanted the perfect woman. . .one who'd fit into my preconceived mold. I thought I needed someone who would radiate with confidence and who'd have the same burning desire I do to share her talents with others by telling them about the Savior."

Tabby nodded. "I was pretty sure you felt that way, and I really couldn't blame you, but it did make me mad. I knew I could never be that perfect woman, so I was angry at you, myself, and even God."

Tears welled up in her dark eyes, and when they ran down her cheeks, Seth reached up to wipe them away with his thumb. "You don't have to be the perfect woman, Tabby. Not for me or anyone else. All God wants is for us to give Him our best." He kneaded the back of his neck, trying to work out the kinks. "I tried to call you last night. I wanted to tell you what God had revealed to me. I was planning to tell you that it didn't matter if you stuttered, had no confidence, or never did ventriloquism again. I just wanted you to know that I love you, and I accept you for the person you are. . .one full of love and compassion."

"Love?" Tabby looked up at him with questioning eyes.

He nodded. "I know we haven't known each other very long, but I really do love you, Tabby."

"But what about Cheryl Stone?"

His brows furrowed. "What about her?"

"After seeing the two of you together, I thought—"

"That we were in love?"

She only nodded in response.

Seth's lips curved into a smile, then he let out a loud whoop.

"What was that for?"

"I don't love Cheryl," Seth said sincerely. He dropped to one knee. "This might seem kind of sudden, and if you need time to think about it, I'll understand." He smiled up at her. "If you wouldn't mind being married to a dummy, I'd sure be honored to make you my wife. After we've had a bit more time to go on a few more dates and get better acquainted," he quickly added.

Tabby trembled slightly. "You—you w–want to marry me?"

Seth reached for her hand and kissed the palm of it. "You're stuttering again. I think maybe I'm a bad influence on you."

She blushed. "I'm just so surprised."

"That I could love you, or that I'd want to marry you?"

"Both." Tabby smiled through her tears. "I love you so much, Seth. I never thought I could be this happy."

"Is that a yes?" he asked hopefully.

She nodded as he stood up again. "Yes! Yes! A thousand times, yes!"

"How about a December wedding? Or is that too soon?"

"December? Why that month?"

"I can't think of a better Christmas present to give myself than you," he said.

She sighed deeply and leaned against his chest. "That only gives us four months to plan a wedding. Do you think we can choose our colors, pick out invitations, order a cake, and get everything else done by then?"

A dimple creased her cheek when he kissed it. "I'm sure we can." There was a long pause, then he whispered, "There is one little thing, though."

"What's that?"

"I don't want our wedding cake to have peanut butter filling."

Tabby pulled back and gave him a curious look.

"My peanut-butter phobia, remember?"

She giggled. "Oh, yes. Now how could I forget something so important?"

Seth bent down and kissed her full on the mouth. When the kiss ended, he grinned.

"What?"

"I must be the most blessed man alive."

"Why's that?"

"If a man is lucky, he finds a wife who can communicate her needs to him. Me. . .well, I'll always know what my wife needs, because she can talk for two." He winked at her. "Now that we've had our little talk, do you still want to go to the park?"

She smiled. "Of course, I do. I can't think of a better place for us to start making plans for our future."

epilogue

Tabby had never been more nervous, yet she'd never felt such a sense of peace before. Next to the day she opened her heart to Christ, today was the most important day in her life.

Much to her sister's disappointment, Tabby had beaten her to the marriage altar. Tabby took no pleasure in this fact, but it did feel pretty wonderful to be married to the man she loved. Lois would find the same joy when it was her turn to walk down the aisle. By then, maybe she'd even be a Christian.

Tabby glanced at her younger sister, sitting beside Mike and her parents at a table near the front of the room. Thanks to Tabby's gentle prodding, Lois had recently started going to church. Now if they could just get her fiancé to attend.

The wedding reception was in full swing, and Tabby and Seth were about to do a joint ventriloquist routine. It was the first time she'd ever done ventriloquism in front of her family. Tabby gazed into her groom's sea-green eyes and smiled. If someone had told her a year ago she'd be standing in front of more than a hundred people, married to a terrific guy like Seth, she'd never have believed them. It still amazed her that she no longer stuttered or was hampered by her shyness. God was so good, and she was glad for the opportunity to serve Him with her new talent.

She felt the warmth of Seth's hand as he placed Rosie into her arms. He probably knew she was a bit nervous about this particular performance. He bent down and pulled Rudy from the trunk. With a reassuring smile, he quickly launched into their routine.

"How do you feel about me being a married man?" Seth asked his dummy.

Rudy's head swiveled toward Tabby. "I can see why you married her, but what's she doin' with a guy like you?"

Before Seth could respond, Rosie piped up with, "Don't talk about Seth that way, Rudy. I think he's real sweet."

"I think so too," Tabby put in.

Rudy snorted. "He's not nearly as sweet as me." The dummy's head moved closer to Tabby. "How 'bout a little kiss to celebrate your wedding day?"

Tabby wiggled her eyebrows up and down. "Well. . ."

"Now, Rudy, what makes you think my wife would want to kiss a dummy?"

Rudy's wooden head snapped back to face Seth. "She kisses you, doesn't she?"

The audience roared, and Tabby felt herself begin to relax. Even Dad was laughing, and Mom was looking at her as though she was the most special person in the whole world. Maybe she wasn't such a disappointment to them after all. Maybe her newfound confidence could even help win her parents to the Lord.

"You know, Seth," Rudy drawled, "I hear tell that once a man ties the knot, his life is never the same."

"In what way?" Seth asked.

"Yeah, in what way?" Rosie echoed.

Rudy's eyes moved from side to side. "For one thing, some women talk too much. What if Tabby starts speaking for you, now that you're married?"

Tabby leaned over and planted a kiss on Rudy's cheek, then did the same to Seth. "Yep," she quipped, "from now on, I'll definitely be talking for two!"

A Letter To Our Readers

Dear Reader:

In order that we might better contribute to your reading enjoyment, we would appreciate your taking a few minutes to respond to the following questions. We welcome your comments and read each form and letter we receive. When completed, please return to the following:

Rebecca Germany, Fiction Editor
Heartsong Presents
PO Box 719
Uhrichsville, Ohio 44683

1. Did you enjoy reading *Talking for Two* by Wanda E. Brunstetter?
   - ❏ Very much! I would like to see more books by this author!
   - ❏ Moderately. I would have enjoyed it more if

_____

_____

2. Are you a member of **Heartsong Presents**? Yes ❏ No ❏
   If no, where did you purchase this book?_____

_____

3. How would you rate, on a scale from 1 (poor) to 5 (superior), the cover design?_____

4. On a scale from 1 (poor) to 10 (superior), please rate the following elements.

   _____ Heroine   _____ Plot

   _____ Hero   _____ Inspirational theme

   _____ Setting   _____ Secondary characters

5. These characters were special because_____

   _____

   _____

6. How has this book inspired your life?_____

   _____

   _____

7. What settings would you like to see covered in future
   Heartsong Presents books?_____

   _____

   _____

8. What are some inspirational themes you would like to see
   treated in future books?_____

   _____

   _____

9. Would you be interested in reading other **Heartsong
   Presents** titles?   Yes ❏   No ❏

10. Please check your age range:
    ❏ Under 18   ❏ 18-24   ❏ 25-34
    ❏ 35-45   ❏ 46-55   ❏ Over 55

Name _____

Occupation _____

Address _____

City _____ State _____ Zip _____

Email _____